under these stars

early praise for *Under These Stars*

"Finally, one of the fellaheen has his say! Tony R. Rodriguez brings a long-needed, authoritative tale of the heroine to Beat oeuvre. His voice is an exciting mix of scholarly and street, a modern sensibility that will jolt readers upright and make them remember they are ALIVE—and all the joy and pain and beauty that comes with it!"

—BRENDA KNIGHT, author of **WOMEN OF THE BEAT GENERATION**

"This is the story of any woman in her twenties with a passion and lust for experiencing the road. It reaffirms the fact/belief that music shapes our lives. UNDER THESE STARS is an honest and unflinching peek into one woman's youthful reflection & self----discovery through the solitude of the open road. Sometimes the answers we seek are within ourselves . . . Look to the stars!"

—TAMMY EALOM, lead singer of DRESSY BESSY

"*Under These Stars* takes the modern day road trip and turns it into an existential journal through the physical and digital landscapes we now cohabitate. It is a 21st century exploration of America if Jack Kerouac were a woman and living in an overexposed media-filled world."

—**CHRISTOPHER CARMONA**, lecturer at the **University of Texas at Brownsville**, and author of **BEAT**

"*Under These Stars* is quite the road trip, brimful of great music, some decent waves, a tasty selection of brews, and a fascinating critique of filmographies that accompany the reader while experiencing a journey of self-reflection and being human. Tony R. Rodriguez writes a sobering speculation of reality."

—**NICH L. PEREZ, CSC**, Holy Cross Brother, **Holy Cross College** at Notre Dame, Indiana

"*Under These Stars* is the literary soundtrack of a modern Beat Generation that copes with a combustible reality they're responsible for shaping. Rodriguez is a clever wordsmith who puts you right in the driver's seat of a life-changing trip."

—**SONNY KILFOYLE**, lead singer of the band **MINKS**

"I have been handed many *Road* books in the last 25 years— this one is on the top of the heap."

—**TOM PETERS**, poet/proprietor at **BEAT BOOK SHOP**

"Surely this is the first published novel to mention Speculative Realism."

—**GRAHAM HARMAN**, author of **TOWARDS SPECULATIVE REALISM**

about Tony R. Rodriguez

"In a confession-booth voice, Rodriguez overflows with pure American Zeitgeist. Listen close—and buckle your literary seat-belt."

—**ERIC DROOKER,** Animation Designer of the film **HOWL** and illustrator of the book **HOWL: A GRAPHIC NOVEL**

"Tony R. Rodriguez has deposited a proverbial elephant in the literary room, having followed it like a Twitter junkie. His books—as timely as hell and as entertaining as heaven—prove that satire is winning the race with reality."

—**PAUL KRASSNER,** author of **CONFESSIONS OF A RAVING, UNREFINED NUT**

Other books by Tony R. Rodriguez:

When I Followed the Elephant

simplicity regurgitated: poems and shorts

Rapid Eye Metaphors

The Disappearance and the Slow Awakening

under these stars

foreword by **ishmael reed**

tony r. rodriguez

published by beatdom books

Under These Stars by Tony R. Rodriguez
San Francisco Bay Area
The United States of America
www.tony-r-rodriguez.com

ISBN 978-0-9569525-8-5

Published in the United States of America
by Beatdom Books
www.beatdom.com
www.books.beatdom.com

for Salvador C. Vazquez,
our Don Chava,
for being the great family man that he was

for that Honky-Tonk Diva,
Kathi Kamen Goldmark,
for reminding us to live life with a song

for the Lawnmower Man,
Jorge Lopez Asencio,
for always reminding me that
the kids are waiting for me at the van

for Gerald Nicosia—
humbly & respectfully—
for all that you've done for BEAT

for the Missing Toe,
that's one gone—
let's not make it two

for Hambone,
I still feel bad—sorry!

and for someone
extra special

foreword
by Ishmael Reed

I've lived through at least three print revolutions since the 1950s, back when I worked in the office of a newspaper as a teenager. Now, there seems to be hundreds of alternatives to the old messy linotype technique. The literary culture, too, has drastically changed. In the 1960s, there still existed many literary publishers for whom the quality of the work was more important than money. This changed sometime in the 1970s, when profits became the rule of thumb for those bottom feeder conglomerates that supplied most of the industry.

Ironically, it was then the government, acting through the National Endowment for the Arts, countered the privatization of literature by funding literary projects, including many literary magazines and journals. In the

1970s, I was elected to the chair of the Coordinating Council of Literary Magazines with Rudolfo "Rudy" Anaya, the late Toni Cade Bambara, Leslie Marmon Silko, and others. We oversaw the funding of dozens of small magazines.

Next came the MFA programs that spawned hundreds of poets, novelists, and essayists. Most of them attended conferences for writers like those sponsored by the Association of Writers & Writing Programs.

Tony R. Rodriguez, however, is a product of the new literary culture. Because there are so many members in its ranks, it's hard to sort them out. But given his talent, Rodriguez would stand out in any literary culture and in any time period.

And though the model for *Under These Stars* is Jack Kerouac's *On the Road*, I find Rodriguez easier to read. (Those who designate Kerouac as a Jazz writer don't know anything about Jazz. It's not to diminish Kerouac's talent to say that he has more in common with the prolix writer Thomas Wolfe than with Charlie Parker.) Rodriguez's Dean Moriarty, cleverly enough, is a woman named Sarah, a young professional who writes for a prominent San Francisco-based literary magazine. She gets into trouble when she buys drinks for an underage celebrity writer. Her "Superior" soon suspends her for a month.

Sarah travels around America in an all-white minivan known as Shadowfax, fitting enough for readers of fantasy. Among those who Sarah encounters include, "Mayumi in Santa Monica; Laney in San Diego; Pearle in Flagstaff; Maryanne in Fort Collins," and many others along the road.

The universal storyline for world literature just might be the classic Hero's Journey, which involves distant travel and many encounters with different characters, an archetypal storyline formula probably dating back to our hunter-gatherer period. Rodriguez, however, boldly crafts his novel to display his road trip hero as a complicated heroine, a literary tactic that pushes aside all those macho male characters of the road proudly contained in our literary canon.

Sarah and her friends discuss films, music and their past college years. In the old days, a college education would guarantee one financial success. But not now when broke college students are found waiting tables, or like Rodriguez's heroine—set adrift in the highly competitive world of writers, which includes more players than ever before in history.

When reflecting on her future endeavors in writing, Sarah offers something all writers have pondered:

> "I toss myself on the couch and sluggishly succumb to my dream world, soon laying subconscious witness to my fancy of being a real writer—a writer people talk about. Someone whose writing gets studied in schools and widely reviewed in syndicated columns. Someone people affirm and critique, for better or worse. Someone who is defended by strangers when critics critique too harshly. Someone who holds public readings in front of eager audiences. I dream that someday I will have published many books in my life, and have participated in many successful interviews of academic merit and artistic awe."

If there is a political world outside of the cyberspace these complex characters of *Under These Stars* inhabit, they are oblivious to it, unlike some of the Beat narratives and poetry, which grafted from some of the values of the proletarian writers of the 1930s. Rather, Rodriguez's characters are more interested in communicating their social happenings through Facebook and Instagram and other forms of social media.

Some of the characters and encounters are quite

compelling, but what attracts me overall is the writing. Rodriguez is capable of original inventions that are often stunning. Whether writing about the mundane or the cosmic, he is always interesting. And speaking as a writer, I could appreciate how much patience and persistence it took to build these textual constructions. This is a remarkable novel from a very gifted novelist, one who tells a story through the eyes of a woman — always a risky thing for male writers. Our collective literary history is littered with failure from such an edgy risk. But still-existing generations now have a better glimpse into this current bizarre and complex culture that is still quite foreign to many.

Under These Stars is one of those moveable feasts that includes drinking, eating, having sex, and moments of speculative wonder.

But, when thinking of Sarah's problematic vice, it's evident to state that there seems to be one thing that unites writers of different generations and different age groups, all across time: alcohol!

A map depicting the protagonist's journey and intended
journey throughout the United States.

disregard objectivity and
tickle wanted subjectivity

1

Here's what I stand by.

He was one of my earthly judges, a brute decider of my shaky future. He had the power to instinctively support me or outright destroy me—bringing me another step closer to hitting the apocalyptic bottom. I sat in front of his well-polished mahogany desk with framed family pictures adorning a fair amount of the desk's perimeter. I was physically paralyzed and emotionally busted, yet still eager to hear how the consequences of my recent actions would soon pan out. My posture was bent like a withered tulip saying its expected farewells. My gaze was nervously fixed on his dark brown eyes, though he was looking elsewhere. I continued to stare at him deeply, without as much as a single blink. He had me in his right hand. He was my Superior.

He dragged up and tapped and distanced his thumb from his index finger in order to expand the contents on the screen of his iPad. Then he pinched his screen and dragged up again. Again. Tapped. Scrolled left. Then zoomed in. My Superior must be carefully studying my yearly online page views, seeing just how many collective hits my past articles had garnered in the calendar year of 2012. There were well over 70,000 hits thus far on my column, something of which I was proud. Those articles—published through our literary journal both online and in print—spoke of my comprehensive interviews with so-called heavy hitters in the literary world. They told of the news I covered first, concerning author meltdowns and classic books at long-last being made into film.

I finally blinked.

Acidy saliva seemingly fermented in my mouth.

My neck and spine tightened and ached from tension.

To my left, seated in a comfy chair, was my web channel's assistant editor, Penelope. Her posture was also bent low, and her index finger and thumb pressed deep into her forehead because of the contagious anxiety permeating our Superior's office. She, too, was paralyzed. She, too, waited to hear our Superior's judgment.

Our Superior put down his iPad, sat up straight, adjusted his ridiculous plaid tweed blazer and stared right back at me, two sets of eyes locked in what seemed to be perpetual intent. There was a disconcerting silence.

Speculative.

Maddening.

Deafening.

Lost.

Beat.

Our Superior leaned forward, cleared his throat, and asked in basic protocol fashion—his voice firm, "Sarah, so tell me what happened."

I then swallowed my saliva, the acidity only partially soothing the dryness in the back of my throat.

Then I blinked again and deteriorated awkwardly into my chair.

Petals were getting ready to fall from this tulip.

2
San Francisco

Dammit. I need to have "the talk" with my boyfriend.

I've widely traveled America's roads and highways and interstates, especially up and down the entire west coast—from south near the Mexican Border, and all the way up north beyond the great Columbia River. And I've come to believe that it's best to get on the road when your heart's eager and young. If you don't attempt to cross America before you hit your thirties, you haven't read much American Literature. Or, perhaps, your travel curiosities mosey elsewhere, or maybe you haven't had the strong yearning to discover your own people, the beautifully bizarre ways and ideals of a culture gone the way of overwhelming awe. That's OK. America understands you'd rather see other parts of the world, parts richer with your preferred scenery and climate, your preferred history of study. Just know that we shape ourselves out on the road, growing further into remarkable souls all plucking down stars well within our reach.

If you're fascinated with America, however, I propose you get on the road quite soon.

I'll soon cross this great country alone—deliberately alone.

I've been with Theo Barnes for almost three months.

We're sitting for breakfast at Pinecrest Diner on the corner of Geary and Mason in San Francisco, just near Union Square. I order the Eggs Benedict and immediately paint the insides of my mouth with the savory hollandaise sauce, my tongue acting as the paintbrush. I feel famished beyond reason—that's what a night of sincere drinking does to us all. Last night was my going away party. Theo and about six other friends came over to my cramped apartment to wish me farewell and safe travels. We laughed and drank and absorbed each other's company in a merriment that would make most binge drinking college kids spiteful.

Theo wrestles a bit in his seat across from me.

My mind is already sailing down Interstate 5, soaking in the land and the wind that'll soon carouse my being and push aside all the past tension and anxiety and frustration that has plagued me over the past week.

For obvious reasons, Theo doesn't want me to go. He tells me this trip will ruin our relationship. He hasn't touched his ham and cheese omelet, and has only appeared to grip his cup of coffee. I've been with Theo for only a short while. I've been faithful, and I'm certain he has as well. He's a damn good man. He's genuine. He's ridiculously handsome, like that of a young George Clooney, or a better-tanned Ryan Gosling or Jude Law.

But I still need to get the heck away from him—and everything else.

I need to meticulously pluck myself from it all. No more daily repetition. No more work. No more anything. Just pure and innocent freedom. And I need to do this road trip on my own. No one else.

About four weeks of personal discovery awaits me.

"You're crazy," Theo whispers to me as he leans over his untouched plate, the ham and cheese wasting away. "You'll be eaten alive . . . The Den of Lions."

I remind Theo that Daniel wasn't eaten by lions.

Theo shakes his head, his right eye squinting with dissatisfaction.

Theo's eyes develop noticeable moisture, and he offers, "I can't be with you."

I put down my fork.

Take a sip of water.

Wipe my mouth.

Lean back.

And I rigidly probe, "How can you be *so* selfish and unsympathetic? Don't you realize what I've just gone

6

through with my profession—this *horrendous* last week of my life?"

Theo says warmly, "I want to be there."

He wipes his first tear.

Theo then babbles poetically and tries to steer the conversation back to our relationship. But I don't let him. He's not as much of a mystic as he'd like to be. There's nothing I can say that will open his ears to my personal needs.

I attempt to speak softly to him with words of assurance.

He mumbles, "What are you going to do out there?"

I tell him it's an organized romp across America, a few weeks of soaking in self-exploration. Nothing more. No fancy gimmicks of flash and flare on my road excursion. I've scheduled a reserved amount of time in each of the cities I'll visit, and I'll be in contact with him often. I tell him I'm Facebooking my entire journey so that he will have access to my daily whereabouts, which I'll try to post regularly. He wants me to sync my smartphone with GPS so he can track my whereabouts in finer detail. I laugh and explain that it's not needed. Facebook will suffice—and it will. Then I sit up with a luminous smile and quickly breakdown my recently devised plan of stops: first, Mayumi in Santa Monica, a sweet old college chum; second, Laney in San Diego, an old high school pal who I kept in good contact with throughout college; third, Pearle in Flagstaff, I don't remember how I met her (maybe first at a party when she once lived in San Francisco), but she's really cool and has been a friend over the years; fourth, Maryanne in Fort

Collins, a current coworker vacationing out in Colorado at her family's nest—Maryanne writes the "Metaphysics" column for our journal—I understand about thirty percent of the stuff she writes, but she gets a shit-load of readers (I've seen the number of page views she generates); fifth, Barbara in Oklahoma City, an old co-worker of mine from my days as a waitress in college; sixth, Jenna in Houston, my lovely aunt who's only twelve years older than me; seventh, Dina in New Orleans, a friend of a friend; and then I zip through the rest of my cross country stops, from West Palm Beach, Florida to New York to Chicago to Fargo and on back to the west coast.

Theo wipes his second tear.

"Maybe I'll start writing."

I don't respond to his slight musing.

With the Eggs Benedict almost gone from my plate and keeping time as a factor, I become succinct and I finish the conversation with Theo.

I tell him how much fun this will be, how much exploration I will experience.

Theo wipes his third tear.

Well, this conversation went better than I had planned.

I raise my right hand to flag our waiter. My hand then flops dutifully like a determined frat boy trying to gain the attention of a bartender in order to purchase just one more round before Last Call.

I question our waiter as he approaches our table: "Can you get the check now, please? We have to go."

Theo is trying his best to stay composed and not let another tear sink down his cold, shaky cheek.

I feel like a strong tulip, one with bright petals and a charming stalk.

3

Theo isn't communicating with me.

He's stoic. He's mechanical. He now scares me.

Theo drops me off on a damp curb a couple blocks away on O'Farrell Street, so I can pick up the mini-van I'm renting. Three days ago, Theo offered me cash to pay for my mini-van rental and driver's insurance. I accepted.

I open the hatchback door of his car to collect the only luggage I'll need: my boogie board in bag with wetsuit, laptop, spare blanket for emergency purposes, and one sizeable duffle bag with my needed basics: 7 pants,

7 shorts, 7 shirts, 7 pairs of socks, 7 panties, 7 bras, 7 scarves, 3 various-sized jackets, 3 sweaters/sweatshirts, 3 hip hats, and other items of personal need, toiletries, and such. I also bring a 300W car cigarette lighter Power AC 110V Converter Adapter with USB Port—just in case I'm somehow stuck in the mini-van and desperately in need to charge my iPhone or laptop.

"Do you have any extra money?"

Theo?

"Anything extra would help."

Theo?

"If you're not going to answer me…"

Theo superficially bites his bottom lip and stares off into the distance.

I start laughing at his melodramatic performance.

He's annoyed and stops biting his lip.

I sling my board across my back, snatch my laptop and blanket, and grab my duffle bag, soon closing the hatchback. Theo then cranks up the stereo and very cautiously pulls away from the curb.

No goodbye kiss.

No farewell.

Nothing.

He thinks he's so cool.

4

I want to begin my American road trip at Ocean Beach. I fill-up the gas tank of my fairly new all-white rental and then stop off at a sandy liquor store near the corner of 4th and Cabrillo. I enter and buy a pint of Gordon's gin. It's OK to drink. I don't mind it. Tastes fine. Today the liquor store has a special on Gordon's gin. Buy one pint for four dollars and ninety-nine cents, and receive a free twelve ounce can of Collins mix. I love Tom Collins. Tastes great. Because of my drunken ways from the night before, and as a creature of habit, I hand the cashier a twenty dollar bill and decide to buy three pints and receive my three free cans of Collins mix. The cashier places my goods into a brown paper bag and asks me if I'd like a red plastic cup for the road. I say yes. He hands me a red cup and no change. I pause and decide whether or not to ask him if he has my change.

Oh, well.

In truth, I've never developed a refined taste for alcohol. It all tastes the same to me. It all gets my mindset to tinker with literary expression.

I hope the same for you.

Ocean Beach.

I find a quiet spot in the beach parking lot and watch the ocean swing dance in imaginative splendor. The waves seem to peak high for this bright non-lunar tide day of summer. Some waves appear to be as high as ten or twelve feet.

I then open a bottle and can, cautiously mixing the two in my red cup.

Soaking in the oceanic beauty, I speculate for a while:

I think I am a good person.

I think I am respectful to all.

I think I can get over the last week of my life.

Many extended moments later, I open another pint and can.

I think I'm doing the right thing.

I think it's important to get on the road.

I think people need to take advantage of their opportunities.

Drunk already.

I want to play on the waves.

I take another deep swig, not quite finishing the second pint or can, and then I begin dressing into my wetsuit on the backseat of the all-white mini-van. A couple of cute men pass by and peep through the front windshield to try and witness my changing endeavor. I drop to the floor in embarrassment. Seconds later, I poke my head high enough to see outside. The two guys continue walking, not once looking back. I slink back to the floor and feel my head begin to spin, but only a little bit. I inhale deeply and make my way out to the distant ocean shoreline with my iPhone and towel in hand and my boogie board bag strapped across my back.

I pause for a moment and post a Facebook check-in at Ocean Beach and contemplate, "Does anyone know their purpose in life?" Then I take an Instagram picture of the rising ocean waves and post it on my Facebook timeline as well. I used the "Kelvin" filter to enhance the image.

I continue on toward the shoreline.

It feels as if I am trudging comically through the sand. There must be people watching me. There must be people around who are laughing at my expense. There must be placers of judgment. We all need placers of judgment. Not too many. But we must have them.

I stop when I'm about twenty yards from the shoreline, the waves beckoning me in their oceanic siren song. I compose myself and build up my posture with what little confidence I now possess. But I'm surprisingly beat. I drop to my knees and decide to rest on my board and take a nap here on the beach. It's only about 10:30 in the morning, so an early catnap on the beach should be fine.

I text Theo, "See you in about four weeks."

I'm fondly thinking of Theo.

Oh, Theo.

So far on Facebook, three people "like" my check-in post. Ten people "like" my ocean photo of rising waves. On my check-in post, my friend Mayumi has commented, "Can't wait to see you, girl."

I lift my head off my board and stare into the lure of ocean waves, those intrinsically sublime curls of beauty. Their song continues in my mind. The coastal wind brings in a slight chill that pushes biting sand up at my face.

I scroll through my iPhone until I reach the YouTube app. I plug into the YouTube search bar "Yo La Tengo Nothing To Hide," and I ease myself into the bitter mood of being alone and buzzing quite well. I soak in the retro video and laugh at the silliness of the band New Times Viking imposing as Yo La Tengo.

I begin to think of the last week of my life.

Then I close my eyes and fall asleep.

5

Penelope was no longer motionless. Her left leg was jumpy. Her posture was now upright. And her breathing seemed to be meditative. Moments before Penelope and I sat before our Superior, the two of us arranged a brief chat in her office. Penelope told me of the severity of my recent actions involving a well-regarded, under-aged writer of immense importance—a recently made giant in the worldwide realm of fantasy.

Penelope told me this offense could lead to my termination.

Penelope said I may have jeopardized the reputation of our publication.

Penelope told me to get my story in order and to speak the sober truth.

Penelope and I are now seated in our Superior's office.

"Well, Sarah," our Superior probed as he set down his iPad.

Our Superior then looked toward Penelope and asked me again, "Well?"

I attempted to strengthen my posture, but the stalk of this tulip was beat.

I shifted my gaze away from my Superior and cleared my throat, the acidic saliva doing its best to soothe the unsettling dryness. My whole body felt like convulsing and becoming lost in an irrepressible rage of apathy. My heart was vehemently ping-ponging inside my chest. My eyes produced a thin veil of saturation. A tear was forming in my left eye. But I dutifully maintained and held that tear at bay.

"Yesterday," I began in a rickety manner, "I was browsing with him in a downtown department store, and then I took him to lunch at a high-rise restaurant over-looking all of Union Square."

"About whom are you speaking?" my Superior pressed.

I failed to answer his question directly. "The interview went well. I scored three publishable zingers in the first ten minutes alone. He was telling me more than I had hoped — even about the adulteress and the misdemeanor."

"Why do you think was he telling you more than you had expected?"

"I think he likes me—quite deeply, actually."

Absolute silence.

Awkward.

Angst.

I could now tell that my Superior wanted me to get right to the point, to only speak in publishable statements.

Penelope interrupted and proposed I tell the full story without interruptions.

Our Superior responded with a final, "Well, Sarah."

6

My iPhone rings, waking me up just a few short moments later. It's McGregor, another colleague at the journal. He couldn't make my party last night due to an urgent deadline that gobbled up his time. McGregor is in marketing. He sells ad space for our literary publication, among other important things that help our journal gain profit. He heard my party was a total smash drive, and he expresses his apologies for not partaking in the celebratory night of excessive libations. McGregor then asks me question after question, but my mind is drifting off into the oceanic distance. The waves continue their sparkly rise and bubbly white collapse, their hypnotic dance. But I do manage to mumble a few disconnected responses, trying my best to get off the phone. McGregor says I should stop by since he lives only a few blocks from Ocean Beach, just near Sloat Boulevard. He says he'll make me a hearty sandwich for the road. After McGregor tosses a few more playful nudges, I agree.

I hang up and check my Facebook. Six other persons have "liked" my recent check-in, and one person commented on my photo, "Ocean Beach is beautiful."

Screw it.

I leave my board and belongings on the sand and I dart toward the water, soon splashing my woozy self into the bitterly frigid waters of the Pacific Ocean. My buzz almost immediately dissipates in the sobering baptism caused by the onrush of the cold and demanding waves. I submerge my body into the biting chill and then slowly rise only to meet the onrush of a falling wave.

Then I leave.

I grab my board and towel and smartphone, slowly making my way to the all-white mini-van. And it's here that I decide to baptize the mini-van. Being that this rental is all-white, I think of something I consider slightly clever. *And now I will name you, and I will call you Shadowfax.* This is done out of respect for the one fantasy writer Who Ruled Them All.

But this Shadowfax will be different. Mine will be a female, an automotive heroine of American-made machinery.

I toss my board into Shadowfax, and then discard the two opened pints of gin, two cans of Collins mix and the red cup into the nearest receptacle. Next, I change into some dry pants and tank top, and finally make my way south onto the sandy Great Highway.

7

I reach McGregor's shabby apartment just off Sloat and 19th. He opens his door and displays a cheesy smile. After smelling the ocean and alcohol mix about my presence, he yanks me in and sits me down on his vintage yet comfy sofa. I don't feel as intoxicated as before—that's what the frigid Pacific Ocean does to inebriated people. But I'm certain that I may appear smashed to McGregor.

"What have you been doing?"

I don't respond.

"Sarah?"

McGregor begins rambling about work and high-pressing deadlines and how our Superior is always coming down hard on him. McGregor feels as if he can never do any good in the eyes of our Superior. McGregor ambles away to the kitchen and pours a tall glass of bottled water with crushed ice. He tells me to drink it, and I can now detect a transformation in his mood. He tells me that if I go on the road smashed like this I'll end up in an accident or in jail. He sits next to me and continues this unexpected lecture for what seems like a few exhausting minutes. I begin to laugh and laugh and laugh, pushing him aside and telling him to calm down.

He asks of my road trip plans.

I spill most of my route in a deliberately rushed approach: Mayumi in Santa Monica; Laney in San Diego; Pearle in Flagstaff; Maryanne in Fort Collins; Barbara in Oklahoma City; Jenna in Houston; Dina in New Orleans; and then I mumbled on specks of my future plans in an even more vague manner.

I don't want to be here anymore.

The clock reads 11:23. *I need to get on the road.* I get up and say thank you. McGregor tries to get me to stay longer—to sober up—but I find my coming here to be more of a distraction. *Shouldn't have come.* He darts into the kitchen like a rogue ninja gifted with stealth and sworn to determination. McGregor tells me to wait until he makes me a sandwich. He says he's making me bologna and cheese. I quickly walk to the front door and again say my thanks and farewells. He jets to the front door, blocking it skillfully with his right arm. With a childlike smile he hands me a bottled water for the road.

I accept his offering and forcefully push his arm aside.

McGregor abruptly, but still delicately, invades my personal space with an unsolicited big bear hug and quick saturated peck on the lips.

"Be safe, Sarah," he tells me as I push him away with both of my elbows and forearms.

"I have a boyfriend, you asshole!"

I slam the door.

No more stalling.

I get inside Shadowfax, toss the bottled water on the back seat, and attach an audio cable to my smartphone, soon plugging the cable into Shadowfax's iPod-ready stereo. The music app on my smartphone contains a substantial playlist I deem proper for my road trip. It houses many illustrious bands of the day: Tennis. Muse. Guster. Vampire Weekend. Fitz & the Tantrums. Of Montreal. Sigur Rós. POP ETC. Best Coast. La Sera. M83. Beach House. Givers. The Limousines. The Virgins. Now, Now. Yo La Tengo. We Were Promised Jetpacks. JD McPherson. Lily Frost. The Naked & Famous. Tunng. Camera Obscura. Tame Impala. Cage the Elephant. Eux Autres. She & Him. The Joy Formidable. Seapony. Grandaddy. Fleet Foxes. The Thrills. The Like. Spoon. Fun. Minks. Dressy Bessy. And well beyond. Should the music app playlist become overused, I can always turn to my Pandora app.

The first song I need to play to officially launch my cross country odyssey is "The Look" by Metronomy—the UK's band of style and promise. And I'm immediately owned by the song's magnetic keyboard melody.

I'm in the musical zone.

I awkwardly sing a paraphrased lyric aloud, "My town's the oldest friend of mine."

I leap eagerly on Interstate 280 south.

Then east across Interstate 380.

Down Highway 101 south.

And then east on the 152.

I need to be clear. You should understand this. My road trip will not focus on seeing America's great and flashy money-pit sites for tourists. Mine is an excursion sharing my reflective existence on the road, wherever the Holiest of Spirits will take me.

8

Theo texts me, "I love you."

He's too much of a romantic—a beat soul lost in some golden age time when love between a man and woman was allegedly perfect, almost fully mystical. It's an anachronism. I know he wants a family someday, a house and children. But I'm not ready for *any* of that. We both graduated from college just about a year ago. I've begun my career endeavors, and he's slowly carving out a path toward reaching his vocational happenings. I think he's working on some crap program to learn how to design websites or something.

We'll see if you love me, Theo.

I want to text him back, but I don't want to text and drive. People die that way. *I'll text him later.* Somewhere around Gilroy, McGregor calls my smartphone—but I don't answer that either.

I stop off at Casa de Fruta once I get about two miles east of the 152 and 156 junction. I check a voicemail message from McGregor wishing me safety and fun times. He doesn't apologize for his rude behavior. I delete the message. I then check-in on Facebook and add a picture on my timeline of apricots accompanied by this message, "These are the world's best dried fancy apricots." And they are.

I browse through Casa de Fruta and then purchase some apricots.

So far, four persons "like" my Facebook check-in at Casa de Fruta, soon followed by two comments on my apricot picture, one comment coming from by my aunt Jenna in Houston.

I begin pounding the dried fancy apricots—and they taste so good.

Back on the road, I soon reach southbound Interstate 5 and decide that I'll need another catnap before long. My energy is spent. And though my recent plunge in the Pacific Ocean appeared to have cured my inebriation, it's now obvious it hadn't.

The gin is finding its way out of my body.

I brazenly veer off I-5 and steer Shadowfax to the side of the road. I open my door and lunge my aching body forward and watch a bit of my pants become instantly saturated with bits of foul smelling apricots—small ponds of pinkish alcohol forming just on the side of the road beneath me. Some of it gets on the lower inside of the driver-side door of Shadowfax. I instantly feel real bad about that. As cars pass violently behind me, I quickly take off my pants and I wipe off the door with some dry patches of cloth not affected by my body's rejection of whatever it was that caused this liquid exorcism. I get back inside Shadowfax, put on a fresh pair of pants, leaving my damaged pants on the roadside.

Wouldn't want a cop to see those pants.

I forget to text Theo as previously considered.

I fight my fatigue and drive on for an hour.

Completely spaced.

Without life.

Or spirit.

Nothing.

As I barrel south along I-5, I lower the passenger-side window and reach about for the untouched pint of Gordon's gin. I grab it and hurl it out into the dry and busted side of the interstate. I crank up the tunes streaming from my smartphone's music app, and I attempt to jet away. I play the entire 2008 self-titled album by Fleet Foxes and drive on until my mind focuses elsewhere.

To places that have echoed in my mind over the past seven days.

9

He liked Macy's. It was his preferred commercial department store. I conducted an important and comprehensive interview as we shuffled through the many store levels of Macy's at Union Square in San Francisco. He told me the whole shebang about his collective literary perils and his recent astonishing successes with book sales, his relational ordeal with his former literary agent, a late twenties-something woman who was at the time married. And on and on to the interview breakthrough concerning his recent police arrest involving his graffiti mural on a SoCal highway depicting two dragons swirling in the ocean-

blue sky. He's such a dragon-loving fool. I want to secretly call him Dragon Boy. Yeah, Dragon Boy! My plan was to publish everything he willingly offered. Soon after the interview, we both decided to grab lunch. My restaurant selection was ideal because it rests above all of Union Square and hails above all those tired souls swirling around just under us in Union Square Park. Once we were seated, he got right to asking me questions about my boyfriend and my dating history. I told him very little. He charmingly begged me to buy a round of drinks—Midori martinis. I'd seen him casually drinking in the photo press twice before, so I didn't mind placing an order to celebrate the soon-to-be success of this interview. The problem, though, was that I had placed an additional two more orders—all three rounds in a little past forty-five minutes. The young author syphoned his drinks from their glasses like it was his life's sole objective. And I followed his lead, holding my own in a celebratory way.

I didn't see a problem with what I did. I was certain he'd been publicly drunk before. It seemed he was handling the excessive alcohol rather well. We soon ate our meal, ravenously. We drank one more round of Midori martinis. He asked for my number as we made our way out of the restaurant, down to the lively sidewalk of Union Square. I gave him a flattered smile and my contact phone number at the journal. And then we soon parted ways—I took a BART train while he took a taxi to his undisclosed residency somewhere in San Francisco.

I thought it was all a success.

The next day I received an email from Penelope stating that his parents were "furiously perturbed" with our publication's choice to intoxicate a minor.

FACTS: The author is twenty years old, almost twenty-one.

Over the past six months various poses of his headshot had been placed everywhere in the literary world. And oftentimes there are also these two widely-circulated pictures of him at a college drinking party or in a park holding a red plastic cup.

My Superior sat forward and went right into it. "So, you've told me that you purchased four rounds of an alcoholic beverage for an under-aged literary icon—and you had watched him drink all four?"

I nodded.

My Superior then expounded that fortunately for me the under-aged author's parents will not be suing or pressing any charges. They had demanded, however, that my recent interview piece must make our journal's front cover. In addition, our journal will also compose a front cover article celebrating their son's literary achievements once a year for three years.

My Superior explained to me that I'm suspended for the next month without pay. My Superior told me that this judgment came directly from the collective board. I am also commanded to have the final draft of my interview first approved by the parents of the under twenty-one icon before publication.

My Superior began quickly typing on his iPad for a good couple of minutes. He then printed two sheets of paper.

An official memorandum.

This is blackmail.

My Superior mandated that I sign at the bottom of the memorandum that specifically discussed this entire ordeal. Penelope signed as a witness, followed by our Superior. He informed me that the memorandum will remain in my personal file indefinitely, and that a copy of this memorandum will be mailed to my residence later today.

"You're excused, Sarah."

Fuck!

Hurriedly, Penelope followed me out of our Superior's office and spoke earnestly that this was a good thing. She, in a somewhat nurturing manner, pleaded that I should somehow count my blessings. She said she'll "look out for me" while I'm gone.

The next day I finished the comprehensive interview and had it approved by both my Superior and the author's vindictive parents, and it was written in a style that I feel was certainly worthy of the front cover. It was speculative yet realistic.

I decide to take to the road during my suspension, have a farewell party, and *not* invite Penelope.

10
Santa Monica

Mayumi is one sexy bitch.

After about two hours more of driving, I become grossly spent. The tunes are still trying to combat my fatigue. I'm getting closer to Santa Monica and my girl Mayumi. I exit I-5 and pull into a gas station parking lot just before the Grapevine. There's a Starbucks on the neighboring side of this parking lot, but I'm in no mood for coffee, despite its caffeinated punch. I need something refreshing. I enter the food depot segment of the gas station and buy an Arizona iced tea tinged with lemonade. The gas in my tank isn't yet dissolved, so I don't purchase any fuel. Back in Shadowfax, I recline my seat and compose myself for a brief catnap. And I dose off in the parking lot. Moments later, I awake due to an erratic beating on my driver-side window. I hear a forties-something woman speaking to some person on her cell. It might be the police given that the woman is now describing Shadowfax and my appearance. I quickly lock the doors and start the min-van. The woman taps on my driver-side window again and tells me my headlights have been on this whole time. I acknowledge her concern, wave back to her with appreciative acknowledgment, and begin to leave the gas station parking lot, soon cruising down the sun-weathered onramp of Interstate 5 south.

I drive for about a good twenty minutes before I feel the shakes come on, my mind wandering while the yawns creep up my chest and out through my mouth. I slam some Arizona iced tea and play some great tunes archived on my music app playlist. Again, I pull off I-5 and make my way to a restaurant, a Jack in the Box, where I utilize the restroom, washing up and such. I grab a ninety-nine cent burger to go and finish half of it before I enter Shadowfax.

Here, I text Theo, "All is well."

He doesn't text back.

I check-in on Facebook and post, "Jack in the Box is good."

No one "likes" or comments on my post.

I call Mayumi and inform her that I should be arriving at her place in well under an hour. The time is nearing

4:45, and my mind and body are purpose driven. *I can't wait to see my girl.*

Soon I exit I-5.

Onto 405 south.

Next over to I-10 west.

Take an exit for 4th Street.

And then straight into the streets of Santa Monica.

I text Mayumi that I'm just down the street.

With La Sera's song "Never Come Around" jamming on the stereo, I pull up to Mayumi's well-tucked away flat near Broadway and 5th Street around 5:25. Mayumi's outside waiting for me. The two of us run to each other as I exit Shadowfax. Mayumi is smoking hot—she hasn't aged since I last saw her about a year ago, her blonde hair still gleaming like ripples of golden undulations, her skin tight and clear, her body curves are pieces of naughty modern art. I grab my duffle bag and laptop, and the two of us make our way into her place. We get right to talking about the old times in college—how we miss living it up as wannabe intellectuals at San Francisco State University. We joke about our many weekend exploits with fascinating men, with our innumerable late night dive bar romps, and our frequent weekend gambling trips to Lake Tahoe and Reno.

Soon an hour passes.

She's a great woman, one full of excitement and vigor.

We then help one another prepare a choice dinner of sliced chicken breasts with rosemary and bacon scalloped potatoes and steamed broccoli bathed in a garlic butter sauce. We sit to eat, and the meal revives my winded body. The entire time our conversation remains youthful and positively electric. Mayumi tells me of her recent success getting hired on as an assistant ad manager with the ABC network, how she'll be in charge of four peers who will all assist her with developing many west coast billboards for ABC's fall television line-up, among many other advertising duties. Mayumi says she's looking into buying some property. Mayumi says she's rocking Zumba three times a week. She says she's awakening her dormant religious side. She says she feels alive. Feels blessed. Feels ripe for the conquering.

Mayumi then asks me of my life, and I give her the one minute teaser version filled with vagaries and disconnected events. She comprehends my choosing to hold back on delving into my life's current issues. Mayumi's enthusiasm is then centered and crestfallen. Her now reserved disposition presents a humble repose. She begins complimenting me on my webpage column, and tells me that my journal is the only literary publication to which she subscribes, let alone reads.

Mayumi heads to her bar in the living room and tells me to join her on her couch. She demands we toss back a cocktail in celebration of my visiting. A few beats later, she hands me a well-shaken cosmopolitan, and we toast to our lasting friendship. I sip the cosmo slowly, thinking about my sickness earlier in the day alongside I-5. I want to tell Mayumi what happened with my queasy stomach, but I don't. I want to purge and tell her of my recent problems with my literary journal, but I don't.

I want to scream.

I scream on the inside.

I scream on the inside again.

Mayumi sets down her drink for a moment and glides across the living room to her 51" flat screen LED 1080p television and tosses in a Blu-ray into her disc player. She starts jumping up and down and comically dancing. Like a host on a trivia show she asks me if I can guess what movie she just put on.

Sex and the City.

"Sex and the City?"

Mayumi offers me a hi-five, and with a heartfelt smile I graciously accept. We laugh and start reciting some of our favorite lines in unison. She joins me on the couch and we again toast with our cosmos in hand.

We continue shooting the shit for about a half hour, our dialogue plump with overwhelming joy and depth and awe. With *Sex and the City* still displayed on the television, Mayumi springs off the couch and proposes we get out of her flat and make a night of it. Mayumi suggests we hit a bar like old times. She says there's one a few blocks away, just down on 4th Street.

"Harvelle's—between Broadway and Santa Monica?" I inquire.

"How did you know?"

"I saw it as I drove up 4th Street toward your place."

"We can *walk* there."

I pause.

"Sure."

A smirk squeezes out onto my lips.

Soon Mayumi shakes us another round of cosmos, to which we both gulp like fruit juice from our youth.

11

The night's young—and in this brilliant moment of existence—so are we.

Together we stroll along the bubbly streets of Santa Monica, soaking in the popcorn lights and the chill coastal breeze and the cheery stars, each pulsating and begging to be noticed. For every attractive and animated male passerby—those who make extended eye contact with us—Mayumi and I smile and seductively wink and blow kisses their way, never once looking back after they pass us and howl their proclamations of attraction and pathetic promises offering spellbinding moments we would never choose to experience in this welcoming night. This is an alluring town. This is a City of Gold—one imploding with social veneration and exuberance and style.

Mayumi and I press farther south down 4th Street, our arms locked and vibrant life circling us in a tornado of mystical wonderment. We soon pass through the musical doors of Harvelle's and become engulfed by the welcoming milieu of red lights. We both stand idle, briefly hypnotized in curious awe by the seductive tunes streaming from the theatric funk band known as the Toledo Show. The band's musical offerings are accompanied by the orgasmic cabaret moves from a few alluring female dancers. Their collective performance is catchy and unrestricted. And there's not even a cover charge tonight. This is a free show. Unbelievable—a free performance! Both Mayumi and I would have gladly paid a cover.

And the Toledo Show really is something else.

Mayumi and I eyeball Harvelle's well-polished extended bar stretching, what seems, well over fifty feet. Harvelle's is packed, though Mayumi and I quickly spot two seats being vacated at the bar. We each frog jump on a barstool and lean forward to get a bartender's attention, and to examine the selections of spirits housed on each shelf. Mayumi tosses a twenty and a ten dollar bill on the bar and asks an attractive approaching bartender for two cosmos with Grey Goose vodka and Cointreau for the triple sec kicker.

He nods at Mayumi—then at me.

Mayumi places her hands on my shoulders and asserts,

"The French produce the best spirits." The eavesdropping bartender smiles to himself.

He's checking us out.

The Toledo Show is bringing the funk.

The bartender hands us our drinks, collects all of Mayumi's money and walks away, not once looking back.

"The rest is for you," she tells the bartender, though he's nowhere close enough to hear her. She hands me the round. We raise our glasses and loosely paraphrase Jack Kerouac's ode published in the ninth chapter of his novel *The Dharma Bums*:

the first is for joy
the second is for gladness
the third is for serenity
the fourth is for madness
the fifth is for ecstasy

We laugh on, and we live on.

Two college souls rekindled in this luminous city.

Another round.

Mayumi insists.

Mayumi pays.

Ah, Mayumi.

We raise our new glasses slowly and carefully and toast to San Francisco State—the university that brought us together; the campus that kept us sane while surrounded

41

by close-minded knuckle-draggers and verbose pseudo-intellectuals; the home where Mayumi and I each accepted our short-comings and hypocrisies and soon grew into the people we are today.

A few handsome men approach us and enter into dialogue. We rudely silence their attempt to converse by laughing at them, then we giggle to one another. We then steer right back to our own conversation.

I soon open up to Mayumi and tell her of Theo.

"I'm not sure if I love him."

"Love's tough."

"It is."

Another round.

Ah, Mayumi.

"I know I treat him like shit."

"Yeah?"

"I don't know why."

"It's tough."

"He tells me he loves me."

Almost an hour passes.

The Toledo Show continues with their film noir soul performance.

We then transition and go on and on about the wonders of life and growing into adulthood. Now pacing my alcohol intake, I confide in her my dealings with the under twenty-one literary icon and my fortunate non-termination. I begin to quietly whimper at the bar. No one notices but Mayumi. I fight back the tears with remarkable success and containment. She tells me to let it out, but I don't. She hugs me and caresses my back, comforting me with gentle words, my troubled head on her left shoulder.

A half hour later, the Toledo Show ends their stellar cabaret performance and we leave Harvelle's, dawdling down the festal streets of Santa Monica like maenads. We lock our arms around each other's shoulders just as we used to do back in college. We look up at the immensity of the shimmering stars stored handsomely within our solar system and beyond. And our stroll becomes paused in potent awe. We pull out our smartphones and open the app named Night Sky. We point out basic constellations and the distant planets of Jupiter and Venus in this fine and clear night sky. We then shout at the stars in foolish drunken fashion. We tell them to turn into diamonds and to fall down to Earth and fill our pockets. We point at our favorite stars and blow kisses at them.

I then tell those stars that I master them.

And they can't look down and judge me.

I'm hungry.

We enter a Hooters near 4th and Santa Monica Boulevard. I order a bacon burger and iced tea. We instinctively laugh at the women exposing themselves inside this popular chain. We stare at each other's breasts and rate ourselves higher than those who must have seemingly manicured their cleavage. We belittle all the waitresses and begin to make up stories about how they each got their job at this restaurant. We go on and on at their expense.

After a short while, we pause.

A few giggles spring here and there.

Soon our smiles dissolve fully from our drunken faces,

and we begin to internally take back all the maliciously vile statements we said about these waitresses merely to satisfy our inebriated fancy. Then we publicly apologize to each other for our harsh words. We consider ourselves good people—but even such people need reminding of the flaws inherently damaging those who may or may not have heard our crude mocking.

We finish our meal and make our way back to Mayumi's place. She opens her front door with some assistance from me. I then dive onto her plush couch, mumbling my goodnights and earnest thanks.

Mayumi tosses a blanket on me. It's a familiar blanket from our past. It bears a cartoon picture of a gator with sweater and hat on, and beneath him is the acronym "SFSU." I used this very blanket whenever I crashed at Mayumi's old place back in our collegiate years of glory. Mayumi shuffles off to the bathroom, unintentionally makes some bizarre and amusing discharge noises, and then navigates herself into her bedroom.

I quietly creep off the couch and snag my laptop. Immediately, I open Microsoft Word and begin hammering literary beats onto the bright screen. I proudly beam as I hear the factory sound of multiple keys being stamped impulsively as I type. I'm writing about my road trip thus far—and it feels great to subdue my worries and lock myself into this craft of swiftly weaving words into sentences that offer contemplation and foolishness and wonder.

I never Facebooked a check-in at Harvelle's or Hooters.

I type more and more and more.

I'm around ten pages into it.
What are you up to, Theo?
Then I fall asleep.

12
San Diego

When I awake in the late morning, breakfast is almost set.

Mayumi is peppy and alert this morning. Together we sit in the kitchen and consume cheesy scrambled eggs and applewood bacon and sweet potato tater tots. *Very nice!* I soon finish the pleasing meal and thank Mayumi for everything. I steal away and shower for a short spell. Then we sit on the couch and watch some television as I pack my things. A Hooters commercial comes on and we both laugh with shame. Mayumi smiles and thanks me for visiting—and for being a great friend. It's time for me to get back on the road.

To push more miles behind me.

To stretch my spirit as far as the road will allow.

To soon become more cognizant of my purpose in life.

I'd love to stay another day or two and soak in more of Santa Monica with Mayumi, but I'm scheduled to see Laney in San Diego by 5:00, and I want to hit some San Diegan waves before then. I'd stay and ride the ocean blue in Santa Monica, but in my experience I've found many surf riders in the Los Angeles area seem to be intolerant of adult boogie boarders, especially those of us from NorCal—but that's merely based off of my own experience.

Mayumi already knows that I have a limited time in Santa Monica. I gather my things and she walks me outside to Shadowfax. I hand her some of my business cards and copies of my headshot advertising myself as a writer. With sympathetic and humbled hands, Mayumi accepts my ads and gives me another hug.

We say our farewells.

"You're going to be just fine in life, Sarah. Don't beat yourself up."

"I'm learning."

And I'm off.

I fill Shadowfax's starved belly with premium gas at a nearby station. I snag a cheap turkey breast sandwich for the road and press forward to I-10 east, then onto I-405 south for a spell, and finally onto I-5 south, soon coasting along the beautiful strip of sandy freeway intermittently running parallel to the vast Pacific blue.

My smartphone goes off, and I let the call go to voicemail. Later, during my bathroom break at a rest stop, I check and discover the call was from the editor of *Illogical Fallacy*, a hip east coast online and print journal specializing in publishing a clever mix of the modern philosophy referred to as Speculative Realism and American Poetry and prose of Speculative Fiction. She wants to talk about the finger-pointing poem I had submitted to the *Fallacy* about American women in 2012. She tells me she's confused and will need some clarity on what I meant in my last stanza. She rambles on into my voicemail that they haven't yet decided on publishing my piece—but she really wants to ask me some questions.

I'll connect with her later.

And I continue sailing south down I-5.

Once I reach San Diego, I take exit 23 toward Balboa Avenue/Garnet Avenue, soon merging onto Mission Bay Drive, then right onto Garnet Avenue until my path eventually reaches Tourmaline Beach—a perfect non-touristy spot free from distractions, a gem of a beach I used to frequent often whenever I visited Laney while still in college.

I spill west down a short hill toward Tourmaline until I rest Shadowfax near the beach bathroom and shower fountains. I call Theo, but he doesn't answer, and it seems his voicemail is disabled. I check-in on Facebook and post a picture using the "Lo-fi" Instagram filter. I add the following text to the post, "Tourmaline is just as I remembered it—beautiful." Then I quickly change into my wetsuit, and then grab my boogie board bag and towel, leaving everything else behind. I find a little place to nest on the beach. I stretch out for a brief moment and prepare my breathing with steadfast focus. Then I grab my board from my bag and attach the hand strap to my left wrist. I walk to the shoreline and put fins on my feet and webbed gloves on each hand to assist me with speed. The waves are breathtaking, serene and alive. It looks as if these Pacific waves are pushing about six or seven feet, with an estimated good thirty to forty seconds of ride time.

And then I'm off.

I walk backwards into the cold water to avoid tripping and faceplanting into the surf. After about fifteen yards, I turn forward, rest my stomach on my board, and press dutifully into the oncoming surf, the breaking waves pushing me back a bit. I weave around gobs of runaway kelp as I push forward. Soon a large forming wave rises before me, promising punishment if I don't position myself appropriately as it passes. I straighten my posture and dive directly into the base of the wave as it folds over me. I kick my fins wildly like an excited dolphin. I press beyond, and with similar challenge, until I reach the farthest set of waves in the distance, the great line-up where the committed surfers and boogie boarders hail. The great line-up floats an estimated forty yards from the Tourmaline shore. In the distance I see a pair of seals mingling in the Pacific blue. The sun above glistens with warm rays plummeting down upon all below who were lost in the twinkly stars from the night before.

13

I swerve along the chill and invigorating surf for a couple of hours or so.

I then make my way back to the shore, refreshed and fulfilled and a bit winded. With a thankful smile, I take off my fins and walk to my beach nest and plop down in its sandy comfort, soon fully stretching out my fatigued body across the warm sand. My breathing becomes reserved and at ease. The sun feels amazing.

And I stay there for a short while, serenely existing in this fine element.

I breathe in deeply and feel my lungs become perfumed with sea air.

The air is sweeter in San Diego.

I'm only now beginning to find inner solace.

Soon, an old woman begins talking to me. She must be in her late seventies. Choosing not to ignore her—though she has interrupted my tranquility—I open my eyes, sit up and submissively squint my tired gaze upon her. The woman possesses sun-scarred skin rich with liver spots, and her scalp has sprouted much ratty gray hair. It's disgusting. I don't want to stare any longer, so I slightly turn away toward the ocean and continue with my squinting. She tells me she was watching me ride. She mentions that I don't ride waves like a San Diegan.

"I'm from the San Francisco Bay."

"NorCal surf riders are more reckless than riders in SoCal."

There's an extended and discomforting pause before she continues.

"What brings you here?"

"I'm visiting a friend."

"Who?"

"Some friend from high school."

"Ah."

Another pause—this one stubborn and seemingly lengthier.

She then goes on to tell me about how great San Diego used to be back in the '80s. She says San Diego is now paradise with lobotomized hoodlums. I tell her that I don't follow. She says the land is still beautiful, but practically everyone here is brain dead, that there's no real life spilling from the beach bums or the bohemians or beyond. I tell her I am here to visit my friend Laney who was a student at USD, who graduated summa cum laude.

She laughs and says, "There are no more true universities in our country no more."

Anymore.

I want to point out her poorly chosen use of the double negative, but I abstain. She goes on and on in that disrespectful and laughable manner, ripping apart anything I say, the two of us never finding any common ground.

I rest my body back on the sand and turn more toward the Pacific blue in a non-verbal sign of annoyance.

Then she plagues me with some thwarting truth.

"You're hurting inside."

She then sits down and asks me if she can read my palm. Irritated, I remain still and endure looking elsewhere. She starts probing deeper and solicits whether or not I'm in trouble.

"You're alone. And the road shouldn't be traveled alone." She tells me I'm on a failing crusade toward my doom. I stand and begin gathering my things in a somewhat rickety manner, perturbed by her offensive ramblings. She persists and tells of her past road trips. As I put my board into its bag, she explains to me how she was once chained to a boulder in Arizona, and she remained there until the arresting police officer received a wire transfer of five thousand dollars from her family. As I fling my towel around my neck, she dribbles on and on about the highway patrol and their wicked ways. I walk quickly away from her, deep through the warm sand. She follows me and speaks of the dangers of driving through Texas.

A nearby surfer with curly blonde hair and a well-built upper-body shouts toward the aged woman with crappy gray hair and liver spots, "Shut up, you gypsy wench!"

I smile and nod in his direction.

He does the same toward me.

The gypsy, the wannabe prognosticator, stops following me and begins lecturing the surfer about San Diego in the '80s. I continue toward the showers as I tell myself not to heed her insolent babble. I put my board in Shadowfax, snag a quick change of clothes and then rinse off the saltwater from my wetsuit in the shower. When done, I peel off my wetsuit and change.

Laney.

My iPhone has two missed texted messages: McGregor and Laney.

I don't even bother to read McGregor's—so I delete it.

I text Laney, "On the way."

14

I soon arrive at her duplex, which is just a bit more east in San Diego's Pacific Beach district. I grab my duffle bag and laptop, knock on the door, and soon see Laney tangled in a web of pain and disloyalty.

Laney's already buzzed. It's evident by her quick yet dragging speech and rosy cheeks and sunset pink eyes, not to mention the open bottle of Malibu rum perched on her coffee table in the living room. The television streams an unfamiliar foreign film starring Javier Bardem, while her stereo is screaming an old track from the Cure, off their

1987 *Kiss Me, Kiss Me, Kiss Me* album, the song being "Just Like Heaven."

Laney dutifully spills her pleasantries and her happiness for seeing me. Then she opens dialogue swollen with apologies for not keeping in closer contact all these years.

I don't say a thing.

I only smile.

I hug her.

Laney then cries madly and falls to the floor, to her knees as she intertwines her fingers in her hands and then bites both of her index fingers in a fit of passionate vexation. Laney wails about another woman, a co-worker, a fornicating whore who slept with her boyfriend David. She begins to tell me everything, tears pouring ferociously down her woeful cheeks, her hands smearing them away only to create new paths for new beat tears to spill down in brutal accord.

She's shaking.

She's falling apart.

She's trying to speak.

"David *says* . . . he *doesn't love* her . . . He *says* . . . *she* pursued him."

I hand her a nearby cloth to absorb her miserable tears.

"I'm sorry, Laney."

Her head's shaking side to side.

"That fucking bitch!"

Laney's broken.

"That fucking whore!"

Laney's spent.

"That *fucking*—"

Laney quickly stands with difficulty and walks in shuddering circles, her face red with rage. She tells me that it just happened. She just caught them at his place— just over an hour ago—just after she had texted me earlier while I was still in the surf.

This is hell for Laney.

I take everything she's saying to heart. I listen as she quickly spills the entire story of David's alleged flirtations over the past couple weeks—of the strange and anonymous messages left in folded notes on his car windshield—of his weird behavior late at night—of the now fathomable genesis of his esoteric interest in her co-worker—the dirty whore. We embrace and I try to calm her. We sit on the couch and she pours a shot of rum into two glasses. I shake my head and ask her to compose herself, to control her tears and her breathing. I lower the television and the stereo, continuing my endeavors to calm her, to be there for her.

"I *want* to call him."

"No, Laney . . . Let's wait . . . Let's *just* wait."

"I'm calling him."

She picks up her smartphone and walks away from the couch, motioning me to stay away.

She's possessed.

She's compulsive.

She's dealing with this shit situation.

David answers and Laney gets right to exposing his character to be nothing more than disloyal gobs of scandalous sludge. I lean back on the couch and close my eyes and lightly shake my head, the frustration growing inside.

Poor Laney.

I feel for her.

This road trip's a mess!

Back in high school, Laney always stood up for me, comforted me, and offered me her loyalty.

She yells into the phone with words now smashed together, as if every word she roared were merged into one super word of hateful exasperation. She needs this release. She needs this purging, this justified attack on the man who massacred her heart.

Laney's words then become more penetrating, more sober, as she asks David, "Where are you?"

I can't possibly comprehend the anguish that she must be suffering.

Laney drops her phone on the floor and collapses next to it as new tears rage, her body contorting into the fetal position of a baby knowing it's about to be aborted. I help her off the floor.

Her body's limp.

Her heart's aborted.

Her tears spill mercilessly.

I drag her on the couch and hug her with the strength of a true friend. Her back shivers on my chest. My right hand calms her wobbly forehead. My left hand clutches her cold left shoulder. She eventually begins to compose herself. Sits upright slowly. Wipes away her tears. Breathes deeply. Wipes her tears again. Breathes deeper. Pours more rum into both glasses, making each a double.

She hands me one and clinks our glasses together.

Laney exhales meditatively.

"We're going out, Sarah."

Laney slowly wiggles her glass then places the rim to her lips, allowing some of the rum to gradually swill down into her quivering stomach. She watches me hold my glass. My eyes zoom deeply into her eyes.

I don't blink.

Time feels frozen.

I don't think I should do this.

Laney throws back her rum.

Laney graduated summa cum laude at USD.

Laney says David is at the slut's home this very moment.

15

Laney lays it all out on the table.

"We *need* to party tonight, Sarah. We *need* to."

This night out is for Laney. For our reunion. For the sake of being young. I finish my hurried shower and change into some evening clothes: knockoff designer blue jeans, tight and revealing black tank top, cute sparkly hairclips, a dark sapphire blue evening jacket, gray scarf and all. I borrow some of her moisturizers and perfumes as she puts on the finishing touches to her evening attire. Laney's smoking hot. I have very attractive friends. I really do. Laney's wearing some tight black khaki pants with an Ann Taylor checkered petite button short sleeve sweater. We both have similar sandals on. I think we look so cute. We really do.

After we finish dolling ourselves up, we spring into Shadowfax and make our way a few blocks south toward Garnet Avenue, then east on Garnet. We're having a night out at the Silver Fox—still Pacific Beach's finest dive.

Arm-in-arm, we walk down a set of stairs and into the bar's main entrance. Laney orders a round of Midori martinis, and I start laughing because that drink now makes me think of my recent interview with the under twenty-one literary celeb, the guy I wish to secretly call Dragon Boy. I then realize that perhaps the double of rum at Laney's was a good idea. *I feel loose.* I need to loosen up more. I've had my mishaps thus far on the road, but those are all now in the past—and one can never alter the past.

We play a game of pool and dismiss every flirtatious guy who makes his snaky way to our pool table. There have been three so far. Laney and I become absorbed in a whimsical dialogue about the flaws in man—as in the *flaws* of male heterosexuals. An attractive male eavesdropper leaps into the conversation sporadically until one of us shoos him away. It's cute to see how hard he's trying.

We finish our game and head to the bar for another martini.

We toast and I begin to feel flirty—but I think of Theo.

"So, I've been with a guy named Theo for about three months, and he's already telling me that he loves me."

60

"Have you slept with him?"

I drop my jaw in shock.

How could she ask that?

"Let's not talk about men."

I agree with Laney.

An attractive Hispanic male methodically sits himself next to Laney. His face is lifeless but still very handsome. He leans forward a few inches and calmly explains to the two of us, "I have had *no luck* with San Diegan women."

Awkward.

Laney laughs immediately.

A confusing smile grows on my lips.

"Ladies, I'm drunk . . . and I am getting the feeling that I have just offended you both. I'm *sorry*." He then walks over to the dartboard on the other side of the dive and begins tossing some darts toward the board alone.

Laney and I get to talking about life in San Diego and such. Our discussion becomes engrossing. I'm having a good time. But every now and then the two of us steal a glance over to the cute Hispanic, one of us at a time. We each individually look his way in a spontaneous manner, and at different intervals—and we occasionally smile at each other because we both know that the other is checking him out. Sometimes I gape for a short while. Sometimes Laney stares for a long while. And vice versa. But our conversation never ceases.

He's not drunk.

He's playing mind-games.

He wants us to be curious.

Laney says she has to go to the bathroom, which

happens to be near the dartboard. She has her drink in hand, and now I know she's full of jive. I watch her as she beelines directly over to the Hispanic, a few hitches in her steps. The two swiftly get to talking. Smiles everywhere. Then some laughter blossoms.

I finish my drink, order two more and make my way over to the flirty dartboard gang. Laney slams her previous drink and graciously accepts the next round from my hand. The Hispanic sneers at me in a cumbersome way and then excuses himself back to the bar.

Awkward again.

"I thought you had to use the restroom."

"What? No, that was *code* that I'm going to chat with that guy." Laney's eyes then gaze back upon the Hispanic.

I think the alcohol is getting to us both.

She continues, "I wouldn't piss in a bar *any*ways."

I laugh.

Laney laughs.

"I'm pretty buzzed right now, Laney . . . Maybe drunk . . . Yeah, I think so. This trip hasn't gone quite the way I thought—"

"You're not drunk, Sarah," she interjects.

Laney walks over to the bar haphazardly, bumping into an unoccupied chair and slightly knocking into people who inadvertently walk through her line of sight.

Laney's smashed.

I need to take charge.

I follow her to the bar and speculate our escape.

Laney gets to the bar and asks the Hispanic for his

name. He tells her he's a poet. I roll my eyes in flummoxed amusement. Laney again asks for his name. He responds with a slow swig of his brew, a Corona Light with a lime wedge practically clogging the neck of his beer bottle. Laney asks for a third time. And he responds that he's a genuine wordsmith, and that he's been writing since third grade.

"You're a writer?" Laney offers as an initial response.

He mumbles under his breath, "I'm a writer. I'm a poet."

And so on.

"You're a writer?" Laney again asks.

I laugh at his pretentiousness. Staring only at his beer, he goes on and on and attempts to recite some of his poetry, but the words can only plop down to the sticky bar floor where they'll remain indefinitely. His words make no sense, and not even in a poetic way. It's horrendous to listen to him recite. My ears start hurting. My stomach feels queasy. But Laney smiles at him all the while.

He then repeats that he's never had any luck with San Diegan women.

I laugh some more, trying to restrain my amusement with difficulty.

Laney siphons a fair amount of her martini and produces a hulking smile.

Her head must be reeling. Her posture seems shifty. And her balance is a tad wobbly.

My slight giggling causes me to become a bit dizzy.

It's time we leave. I grab Laney by the arm and nudge her toward the exit of the Silver Fox.

"What are you doing, Sarah?"

The Hispanic continues running his mouth, splattering his dumb words across the bar. *Screw this.* I reach into my purse and pluck about twenty of my business cards and toss them at the charlatan drunkard, the wannabe poet who must have never even bothered to study the craft of poetry. Laney begins chuckling to herself.

The Hispanic laughs at my face.

He stands from his seat and applauds wildly.

He then holds up a few business cards in his hands.

The bartender shouts toward a security guard in the back of the bar and points to the Hispanic, signaling to the security guard that he needs to eject the failed slob of a writer.

Laney takes another drink of her martini and continues laughing. I tug her again toward the exit. She nods in agreement. We put our glasses down on the bar and walk up the entrance stairs and leave.

Without using the crosswalk, Laney and I dart toward Shadowfax, parked directly across the street in a shopping center, cars honking as we jaywalk to the other side of Garnet Avenue.

I'm not confident I should drive.

"Start the damn car, Sarah."

I tell myself, *I'll be fine.*

Laney's hungry. She then instructs me to head west down Garnet toward Jewell Street. Then make a right on Ingraham. Continuing on as Ingraham turns into Foothill. Then on to where Foothill becomes Turquoise. We arrive at a tiny all-night burrito spot called Los Dos Pedros, another shiny token of Pacific Beach magic.

I order a California breakfast burrito with extra avocado and a soda. Laney orders the same. We eat our burritos and laugh and have a fine time discussing the new friend we had just met at the Silver Fox.

16

Eye boogers don't bother me.

I'm so hung over.

I check a clock on the wall near Laney's television. It's a circular wooden artifact with bronze hands. After I collect that it's 11:23 in the *ante meridiem*, I pick myself up off her couch and flick an eye booger well across the room. Sure, it may not be ladylike or respectful in any means whatsoever, but it had to be done.

I snoop around Laney's place, just to be nosey: I gently browse around her living room; with stealth I read every title in her massive DVD/Blu-ray collection, top to bottom, left to right; I tiptoe to her kitchen and browse the contents of her cabinets; through her fridge; through her pantry; her bathroom medicine cabinet; and then I find myself in front of her bedroom door.

I decide to no longer browse.

"Laney, you up?"

"More hours."

"Pardon?"

"Tired."

"Oh."

I go directly to one of her kitchen cabinets, the first one to the right of her refrigerator and grab the largest glass cup she owns. I open the fridge and pour myself a hearty glass of orange juice, filling it to the near top of the glass. I grab my laptop and walk back to the living room couch, turning the television on to the Cooking Channel.

I open my laptop and plug in the battery charger.

I swipe along the built-in mouse pad to waken the laptop.

I then resume the memoir narrative of my American road trip.

17

The wooden artifact reads 1:23 in the *post meridiem*.

"Saaaaarah, oh Sarah—Ohhhhhh! So tired!"

"Good morning."

Laney creeps toward me with soft and playful steps. She walks over to the couch and shakes the top of my head, moving my hair in all directions. She soon disappears into the kitchen.

I drink the last of my orange juice and continue punching keys down on my laptop, the ticking sound rhythm feels mechanical and industrious. Since I began typing this morning, I must have cleared close to twelve pages, maybe thirteen pages of prose.

Yes—thirteen.

The Microsoft Word page counter at the bottom left-hand of my laptop's screen states, "Page: 23 of 23." This includes the previous ten pages I wrote earlier while at Mayumi's house.

Laney comically bunny hops into the living room and questions, "Would you care for some fresh just-add-water buttermilk pancakes with generic chocolate chips?"

"Do you have syrup?"

"Aunt Jemima."

"Three please!"

I close my laptop and pluck some needed basics from my duffle bag, making my way back to the bathroom to shower and freshen up. In the shower, I remind myself that I need to connect with the editor of *Illogical Fallacy*.

I'll call later.

Soon enough, Laney and I are seated at her quaint kitchen table. The pancakes hit the spot in a most gracious way. We laugh at each other and shake our heads as we summarize the limited yet bizarre events that previously transpired at the Silver Fox.

Then we talk some more.

We talk of Theo.

We talk of David.

We talk of our senior year in high school.

We talk of Laney's future without her ex-boyfriend.

I tell Laney of the interview slip that almost meant my job.

18

Laney decides it might be best if she again napped. Our absorbing and meaningful conversation spanned just under a couple of hours—quite engaging. We're both still spent.

I toss myself on the couch and sluggishly succumb to my dream world, soon laying subconscious witness to my fancy of being a real writer—a writer people talk about. Someone whose writing gets studied in schools and widely reviewed in syndicated columns. Someone people affirm and critique, for better or worse. Someone who is defended by strangers when critics critique too harshly. Someone who holds public readings in front of eager audiences. I dream that someday I will have published many books in my life, and have participated in many successful interviews of academic and artistic merit.

"Wake up, Sarah." Laney drags me back to reality.

She's standing above my rested body and holding two glasses of orange juice. "So, what do you want to do today — tonight?"

"Let's see a film and have dinner."

"Perfect, Sarah."

Laney floats a smile at me.

I'm glad we're not hitting a bar.

I stretch and sit up straight, wiping away the continuous sleepiness that has infected my body. I wipe my eyes and feel no eye boogers. I open my laptop and begin checking nearby theaters for films and show times. Laney's still holding both glasses of orange juice.

"*Snow White and the Huntsman?*"

"No."

"*Men in Black III?*"

"No."

"*Prometheus?*"

"No."

I pause.

"How about seeing *Moonrise Kingdom?*"

"That's the one, Sarah! I love Wes Anderson's films."

"It's at the AMC Mission Valley 20 at 4:30, 5:30, 7:15, 8:15, and 10:10."

"Sarah, I say we view the 7:15 showing and grab

71

dinner just before."

"I'm in."

I float a smile back her way.

She hands me some orange juice.

19

Dinner was satisfying yet uneventful. We should have gone to Moondoggies on Garnet.

We then soak in *Moonrise Kingdom.*

As soon as the closing credits begin to project, I pull out my smartphone and open Twitter and tweet: "Wes Anderson is stellar—his directing is so playfully artsy and chic."

I only use Twitter to tweet movie reviews under @fieryfilmgal. I have over 12 thousand followers. It's pretty cool.

As we leave the theater, we go on and on about the film's youthful story and how well each actor performed in their suspiciously dead-on roles.

I tweet again: "The writing duet of Wes Anderson and Roman Coppola created playful electricity when they composed the script for *Moonrise Kingdom*."

And again: "The script is flawless and offers audiences a high range of quality dialogue and plot and subplot development."

Again: "The script presents children behaving as adults and adults finding themselves in childlike situations. Compelling and masterful."

Again: "The relentlessly quirky ways offered in the film make spectators notice the genius behind the narrative composed by Anderson and Coppola."

Finally: "Best film of 2012's summer breeze."

I hashtag #MoonriseKingdom and #WesAnderson where not restricted by the 140 character limit.

We drive back to Laney's, plant ourselves on her couch and zone out on some more quality programming offered on the Cooking Channel.

We get sleepy.

We call it a night.

We both sleep with welcomed ease.

I awake and see the wooden artifact bare 8:35. I quietly begin packing my things while Laney remains in slumber.

Soon she wakes and sees that I am packed and set to hit the road. Laney demands we grab a quick bite at the Denny's on the corner of Garnet and Mission Boulevard.

Laney chooses to eat light, while I choose to fill up my belly with a sizeable skillet containing gobs of proteins and carbs. Laney pays the bill and we then make our way back to her duplex.

We embrace.

We smile into one another.

We offer kind words of departure.

I collect a good stack of business cards and headshots and hand them to Laney.

Laney pauses and offers back, "You were always sharper than me, Sarah."

I laugh quietly to myself.

And I'm off.

The weather is hot—almost brutal. Making my route toward I-5, I begin searching for the air conditioning button. I can't figure out the AC. None of the buttons seem to be the correct AC button. An LCD screen on the dash of Shadowfax reads the outside temperature to be eighty-nine degrees Fahrenheit, and it's only about 10:30 in the morning.

I press east on Garnet Avenue toward Lamont Street, where I make a right. I replenish Shadowfax's belly at a gas station just at the corner of Lamont and Grand.

My eyes wander everywhere about the gas station. I see an attractive Scandinavian-looking male in perhaps his mid-twenties pushing a stroller in the immense heat. He makes his way to a shady spot near a public phone and dumpster. I find myself staring in wonder.

It seems the Scandinavian makes eye contact with me. Our gaze is locked. I smile at him, and he smiles back.

Who's he? I look away. Seconds later, I look back. He's still staring at me. He deepens his grin and begins pushing his stroller toward Shadowfax. He reaches my door. I speak first.

"You have a beautiful son."

"You look real familiar."

"I don't know you."

He starts laughing toward his child.

He starts rocking the stroller back and forth.

He looks deeply into my eyes and shamefully questions, "Do you have any money?"

I reach into my purse and offer him a five dollar bill.

I rev up Shadowfax and drive away east on Grand. The Scandinavian waves farewell to me as I gaze into the rearview. I then steer onto Mission Bay Drive, finally taking the onramp onto I-5 south. I'm only on I-5 for a short while, soon merging onto I-8 east toward the Arizona border.

20
Phoenix

The heat is unbearable.

I cruise east along I-8 and notice that most of the greenery of land has evaporated along the roadside and throughout the greater landscape. When the landscape is lush with green hills and swaying trees and other forms of effervescent life, there's a reflective purpose at hand — a purpose many choose to not contemplate. Most fail to appreciate the roadside beauty painted across our country like complex green brushstrokes far too esoteric to divulge reason. Farther east along I-8, the land morphs into a shade of brown that seems to have never known rainfall. Soon most of the road signs slowly dissipate along this forsaken strip of beat interstate. Road signs remind drivers of speed limits and mileage toward cities of destination—signaling that you're a part of civilization—these signs are now becoming even more and more scant.

Then I-8 drags you south near the Mexico border, two countries lip-locked in geographic tension. Here the land is flattened and barren with only the skeletons of telephone poles and telephone wire perpetually sending signals out into the greater abyss. The land is now a lighter shade of brown, reminding us all that hardly anything grows in this kind of desert. The dash of Shadowfax reads the temperature to be ninety-six degrees Fahrenheit. I fumble again with the dashboard control buttons—but I still can't figure out the air conditioning system. I don't see any buttons displaying "AC" or "A/C" or a possible "snowflake" symbol.

I feel dumb.

I get frustrated, so I switch gears in mood. I tough out the demanding heat and plug in my iPhone, shuffle to my music app and play the entire *Passive Me, Aggressive You* album by the New Zealand post-punk revival band the Naked and Famous.

And I'm lost.

And I'm beat.

And I'm here.

And I'm speculating the road to come.

Farther and farther, I see the land continue to vampire

the sparse life out of the scenery and beyond. I rack up the miles eastward. For a spell, it seems even the dead brown earth begins to fade away into an ungodly color of tannish white. I'm now just about a dozen miles away from the Arizona border.

Ninety-nine degrees.

No one's on the road. I squint forward and see no cars coming toward me on the opposite side of I-8. My rearview mirror displays no cars behind me for what appears to be miles. The land remains flat and dead.

Where're the traffic signs?

Where're the telephone poles?

Where're the telephone wires?

I feel removed from civilization.

I soon reach what I assume is a Department of Homeland Security's Customs and Border Protection inspection stop, just near the California/Arizona/Mexico border, on I-8 near the edge of the town of Yuma. This isn't a border *crossing* inspection stop. I'm assuming it's more of a stop that inspects on behalf of national security, namely monitoring whether or not illegal immigrants are attempting to migrate deeper into the country.

I slow Shadowfax's speed to around five miles an hour and creep through the first section of the border patrol inspection stop. Three border agents stand under a building with a small awning providing modest shade. They all appear to gape at me from behind their dark sunglasses—their lips contorting into fiendish smiles. I see no other cars at the stop. No cars in front of me on the road. No cars behind. *I feel weird.* No guard stops me at this first sector. I continue on about thirty yards in my ongoing slow approach, and I now enter the second and last check point before the rest of the road opens up to freedom. I steer Shadowfax to an even slower pace. This section has close to six customs-border agents, all with similar dark glasses. All but two sit in chairs. Two are holding black shotgun rifles with pump action. This image makes me feel weirder. I quickly imagine tiny bullets releasing from an echoing shotgun boom.

A suspicious guard gets out of his chair and walks quickly up to Shadowfax's glass face. He taps on the windshield and commands, "Halt!"

I do.

I roll down my window halfway.

"Declare citizenship."

"American—from San Francisco—I live in the Mission District—just near the corner of Mission and 24th."

He motions me to fully roll down my driver-side window.

He pokes his nose inside Shadowfax and asks to see my identification. I hand him my ID. Another agent assists him and inspects Shadowfax by looking through the back windshield.

More nervousness infects my insides.

"Where you going, woman?"

I speak quickly.

"Visiting-friends-my-friend-Pearle-who-lives-in-Flagstaff-and-my-co-worker-Maryanne-who-lives-more-north-in-Fort-Collins-in-Colorado-and-um-um-Barbara--in-Oklahoma-City-and-then-Jenna-in-Houston-she's-my-auntie-and-Dina-in-New-Orleans."

I mumble on until he stares away and motions me to quit talking.

Then he probes, "You're alone?"

"Yes."

He hands me my ID and nods, "You be careful now."

He signals me to press on.

And I drive.

Freedom.

I'm slowly entering into a different time zone. I'm now in Mountain Time. I've lost an hour of my day.

The nervousness expels its nasty being from my body. I play the entire *Passive Me, Aggressive You* album a second time as I cruise through scenery slowly growing greener as the road beelines and twists and then rocks and then rolls. I feel liberated. I-8 steers me through the towns of Mohawk and Theba and Big Horn and Casa Grande. It's through Casa Grande where I approach a sizeable overpass and see close to ten people in tank tops and short shorts, all presenting the colors of our American empire. These beautiful people each wave signs pleading the cruising motorists below to honk for a flash of plump American breasts.

I honk wildly.

As I'm about to pass under the overpass, I witness a cute male holding up a sign that mandates, "Keep Driving!"

I see another sign that reads, "Don't stop."

I pass fully under the overpass and look in my rearview to see one blonde woman turn and run to the opposite side of the overpass to expose her sizeable breasts toward me. Bouncy laughter and dignified applause leap from my now celebratory demeanor.

I turn up the volume when I hear the song "Young Blood" by the Naked and Famous. And I'm lost in the spell of musical hypnotism.

I drive through Casa Grande until I merge onto I-10 east, eventually reaching Phoenix around 4:30. I take a random off ramp and zigzag toward the big buildings of downtown in a most eager way, soon reaching downtown, specifically the corner of North 1st Avenue and West Van Buren Street, just near the Phoenix City Government Building and the Federal Building on the adjacent corner. I drive and drive around the big buildings aimlessly. *It's so hot.* Despite the brutal heat, I need to park somewhere and stretch out. But there's no place to park unless I pay for parking.

Hundred and two degrees.

I drive away from the downtown buildings and wander back east toward the interstate. I stop off at Alamo Mart on the corner of East Van Buren and North 20th Street. I buy three bottled raspberry lemonade drinks and get back behind the wheel of Shadowfax, and I fumble more with the buttons on Shadowfax. *Shit!* I still can't figure out the air conditioning unit. I slowly get back on the road and saturate my parched mouth with the raspberry lemonade. I pound a whole bottle. *Oh yes!* I drive a bit north on 20th Street and stop off at Edison Park, an open space of somewhat flattened and dying public land with about twenty palm trees scattered with little purpose. I find a place to park Shadowfax for free and I walk around the park with a new bottle of raspberry lemonade.

I check-in on Facebook and post a picture of this fading park.

The late afternoon heat continues to be unbearable. It consumes me fully like a fiery furnace. There's no one at this park except an elderly woman sitting on a bench that's withered by many seasons.

I approach her and ask if I may have a seat next to her.

She asks me if I'm going to harm her. She asks me if I know her. She asks me what I want. I remain quiet and unassuming. *Nothing.* She tells me her name and everything she's currently going through in her golden years. She tells me that I need to help her. She says she misses her husband who passed away a few years back. She asks me to sit down. I do. She tells me that she wants to die. I put my arms around her and gently squeeze.

"You're going to be fine in life."

"I am," she acknowledges.

I reach into my purse and offer her a few business cards. She accepts them.

I walk away and finish my second raspberry lemonade.

21

Back in Shadowfax, I mingle my way onto Interstate 17 and press on north for an hour or so, drinking some more raspberry lemonade in order to maintain some level of combating the lingering heat.

My iPhone goes off somewhere around Camp Verde. I check the screen and see Penelope's trying to reach me. I don't answer. She leaves a voicemail. I finish my third raspberry lemonade and soon pull off I-17 to take a restroom break at a gas station, fill-up Shadowfax, grab another bottle of juice and check my message from

Penelope. The message informs me of bizarre events at the journal.

I call Penelope and she confirms the items she stated in my voicemail: McGregor suddenly quit our literary journal; and the under-aged, dragon-loving literary celeb with a knack for writing fantasy has left many messages on my personal voicemail at the journal, and he's even left messages with Penelope.

I'm really going to call him Dragon Boy.

Penelope said I should call him soon. I tell her I'm not calling anyone. I say thanks and end the call.

Before continuing on toward Flagstaff, I remember that I need to finally phone the editor of *Illogical Fallacy*. The time on the east coast must be rather late, but I choose to call anyway and leave a message. I keep it short, pretty much informing them that I'm on the road and they have my permission to edit my poetry as they see fit.

I then call Pearle in Flagstaff. She doesn't answer her cellphone, so I call her at home. No one picks up. I leave a message on her home phone messaging system to let her know that I should be arriving in Flagstaff in an hour or so, possibly around 7:00 this evening.

I start up Shadowfax and journey farther north, pushing back the miles. More greenery appears along the landscape as I drive. The rolling hills here possess more life. The sun continues to slowly descend. The air is cooling, though still in the high eighties.

Around 7:15, I reach Flagstaff, seeing the city lights beginning their twinkly dance in this gorgeous early evening moment of existence.

22
Flagstaff

I pull into Flagstaff where I-17 merges into South Milton Road, just near Northern Arizona University. I think of my studies at San Francisco State University. I think of my various courses analyzing American Literature. My eyes then spy across the campus of Northern Arizona, and I see a name on one of the university's buildings. It says "Philosophy" in large black font. For some odd reason I think of the concept in modern philosophy known as "Speculative Realism." I was introduced to this philosophy at SFSU.

My mind shifts.

Feeling a bit hungry, I stop off at a Chipotle Mexican Grill near the corner of South Milton Road and South Plaza Way. I enter the restaurant and move to the side of the line before I order. I call Pearle again. No answer on her cellphone or home phone. I leave another message on her home machine.

Grilled chicken burrito with white rice and black beans, roasted chili-corn salsa, sour cream and cheese, with a three-finger pinch of additional cilantro.

I take my time eating.

I ponder my entire trip thus far.

I think about Theo and my job situation.

What should I do now?

I exit Chipotle and sit in Shadowfax, dazing off for a while. It's now a little before 8:00. The rays of sun are now only spare shards of gold, a remnant of solar rays offering their last direct collection of radiant pulses. The exodus of light will soon engulf all in a beautifully poetic way, the moon providing the only brilliant light to be digested by the human eye. I take out my laptop and begin editing the twenty-three pages of prose I've conducted thus far in my road trip memoir. My edits are focusing on shortening my non-poetic sentences of passable length, chipping away at failed adjectives and adverbs and the laughable syntax I vomited on the screen in certain sections.

My iPhone goes off. Theo's calling. It's close to 8:45. The sun is long gone. I pick up the phone and stare at the screen. *I don't think I love him.* Then I put my smartphone down and stare at its screen. Theo doesn't leave a message. I try Pearle again, leaving another message on her home phone, and then my first message on her cellphone messaging system.

Screw it.

I drive around aimlessly, all throughout Flagstaff: down Route 66; to South Woodlands Village Boulevard; down South Plaza Way; then up on South Yale Street; east down South Mertz Walk; then into bizarre patterns of road I'll choose to pass on sharing. I wander stupidly.

I find myself back on South Milton Road, somewhere near a gas station. I pull into the gas station parking lot off to the side, just near the water and air pumps. A drunken Native American approaches Shadowfax with slow, draggy steps. He's about twelve feet away. He begins blathering incoherent nothings. I immediately wonder if I am foolishly mistaking his drivel for perhaps his native tongue. After about ten seconds of trying to comprehend his rambling poppycock, he drags his bitter legs a few feet closer. I become uneasy. *This man is smashed.* He then groans his inebriated nothings toward me as I choose to roll-up all of the windows. I turn away and pretend I'm working on my laptop. He then hauls himself to Shadowfax and starts tapping softly on my driver-side window, babbling out more of his dribbled words never to be recognized by coherent English speakers.

He shows me his hands, which appear to house deep lacerations still struggling to heal. They're infected and perhaps induced by hard manual labor.

He begins banging hard on my window, still spilling

out his incomprehensible woes.

I start Shadowfax and slowly drive away, seeing him in the rearview mirror.

What the hell?

It's about 9:30 when I reach an America's Best Inn just at 910 South Milton. I pull into the parking lot. I need a place to stay just in case Pearle flakes on me. I park Shadowfax and enter the office. I instantly become friendly with the motel manager, a young man named Malik Sharma. He tells me many things. We get to talking about politics and religion. I know nothing, so I choose to remain quiet as he lectures about our nation's current state of affairs—national debt, foreign enemies, the Second Amendment, and on and on.

I notice framed pictures on his wall of quasi-famous people who've stayed at his inn. I offer Malik a headshot and some business cards—and he promises he'll display them immediately on his counter, then later frame the headshot and put it on his wall. He asks me to sign the headshot.

I do.

He then shoots me a few names of hip dives in the area.

I'm not staying in.

I go to one named Bun Huggers Lounge nearby on South Milton Road. One of the locals, a beautiful dirty blonde college girl, a student at the university, tells me they have great burgers. I order a beer, pass on a burger, and soon meet a guy named Henry, a decent looking fellow in what seems to be his mid-thirties, regal face.

We start talking. I'm taking small sips of my beer while Henry throws back his rounds like a sexually-repressed groomsman during a Las Vegas bachelor party peep show. He's not flirting with me. He's just talking to me. I think he just needs someone to confide in. Something might be going wrong in his life. He stops ordering drinks for himself. We then share moments of stale silence. He then dissolves the silence and asks if I'd like to have a cigarette outside the bar to help him sober up. I don't smoke, but I go anyway. Gentlemanly, he escorts me outside of the bar, just in front of the main entrance. He puts a cigarette to his lips and then puts his right arm around me. I push him away and tell him I have a boyfriend. He starts laughing with his unlit cigarette dangling from his lips. He calls me a dirty little dyke. He tells me that I'm a liar. He says my boyfriend is stupid for letting me out alone. I get nervous. Someone may hear this confrontation. I storm directly toward Shadowfax, get in, lock the doors, and drive out of the parking lot.

I make my way back to the inn, trying to avoid being seen through the front office window by Malik. But he sees me anyway. We make eye contact. I notice he has already set up my headshot and my business cards on his counter. He quickly pokes his head out of the front office door and shouts at me.

"Did you enjoy yourself?"

"Great."

I give him a comedic salute and wave goodbye.

Where's Pearle?

I grab my duffle bag and laptop from Shadowfax and

enter my room, heading straight for the bathroom where I turn on the lights and drop to the floor, my knees before the toilet—the toilet seat is down. I cry and cry. I check my iPhone and see that I have no missed calls. I open Facebook—and then close it immediately. Leaving the bathroom, I toss my body onto the queen-sized bed and cry some more, punching my fists at the pillows, wiping my tears on the comforter. I become restless. I think of many things.

I speculate my reality.

I flip on the television and fumble through the channels until I reach HBO, which just so happens to be showing the 1999 hit literary film *Wonder Boys*. Nearing the end of the film my eyes become sleepy, and I'm about to gently float away to the netherworld of dreams where I'm free to imagine that I'm a *Wonder Boy* type of writer, one who may get discovered by a much larger audience.

And so I'm dreaming—again.

23

I wake up in the early morning to find Pearle has left me three messages on my voicemail. I call her back and listen to her apologies machine-gunning my ears. She feels awful. We meet at an IHOP on South Woodlands Village Boulevard and we get to talking about what happened last night. Pearle looks busted. Real busted. It's as if she's just gotten back from an all-night clambake with Charlie Sheen and the boys. Pearle doesn't look much like she used to back when she lived in San Francisco. She's definitely a Facebooker who rarely publishes current pictures of herself.

Pearle laughs at my story of the inebriated Native American. She slaps her palms on the table when I tell her about Henry and our scene outside the Bun Huggers Lounge. Then I tell her of America's Best Inn. Pearle returns with her apologies. She goes into this long whopper about how her boyfriend gave her crap yesterday. They fought. She pushed him. He threated to smack her. She kicked him out of her place. They made up hours later. They fought again. They made up. They made love. But Pearle didn't use the word "love."

And on and on and on.

Pearle's changed.

I overhear a couple of elderly ladies in the booth behind me bickering about some of their family members who are either hoarders or wasters. Their words are irate and disturbing. I eavesdrop on their conversations as Pearle goes on and on about her boyfriend.

How he's a keeper —*despite it all.*

How he's attracted to her —*emotionally.*

How he makes her feel good —*about herself.*

Pearle abruptly shifts her performance in bipolar fashion, soon entering into a state of serious consciousness. I focus my attention back on her as she asks me if we can go to her place after breakfast and settle in.

I slowly pick at whatever-it-was-that-I-ordered and tell her I need to move on. *Nothing personal.* But I am done here. Flagstaff was kind to me, except, of course, Henry and the Native American derelict. I need to hit the road.

Pearle laughs despite her failure to comprehend my

sentiment. I tell her all is fine, but inside I'm still pretty bruised by her actions. She again apologizes, soon leaving IHOP without even chipping in any money for the bill.

She ate breakfast, too.

She even ordered both coffee and orange juice.

I should have known when she asked for double the skillet meat.

I decide to stay in the booth for a while, alone.

I ask the waitress for a piece of paper and a stamped envelope, but only if she could spare it. I tell her I'll pay for the postage on my bill or pay on the side in cash if she prefers it. She smiles and explains that it will not be necessary. She then informs me that the paper and envelope will be on IHOP stationary. I say that's fine. When she returns, I begin writing a letter to Theo. I tell him sweet things. I speak the sober truth. Then I make stuff up. I get lost in a rhythm of fun-sounding and poetic words. It's like I'm in junior high and I'm informing Theo of things I have never said before. It feels good to write these things, fictitious or not.

I decide to leave and get back on the road.

I leave a business card behind with the paid bill.

I go back to America's Best Inn and pack my things. I say goodbye to Malik as I check out. He smiles when he asks me if I liked his establishment. I obediently smile and nod. He points behind me and motions to where my headshot is hammered proudly on his wall. Malik has already put up my framed headshot with signature—and now the number of the room I stayed in is also listed on my headshot.

Imaginatively, I'm now quasi-famous.

I make my way out of the parking lot and aimlessly drive around Flagstaff, soaking in all the natural beauty. I feel earthy. In many parts of the city, there are trees ubiquitously proud.

I fill-up Shadowfax at a nearby gas station and use the restroom, soon leaving and making my way toward the highway. I stop at a mailbox I spot on a side street. I want to deliver the IHOP letter to Theo. I park and mail the letter, soon getting back into Shadowfax. A little boy peddles up on his BMX bike and says hello. I roll down the driver-side window and ask him why he's not in school. He says there's no school today. He tells me it's Saturday.

I check the calendar on my iPhone. It is Saturday. *Shit.*

He tells me that I look funny. *I look funny—you brat!*

I tell him I'm not from here. *I'm from California.*

He examines Shadowfax, offering such a response, "Never been to California."

Awkward silence.

I roll up the window and drive away, not even bothering to look back at that little weirdo.

24
The Four Corners

I'm dying.

Too much driving.

I make my way slowly onto North Switzer Canyon Drive; soon north onto US-89; then east on US-160, the Navajo Trail; sixty-plus miles later, I take a short left onto New Mexico Highway 597, where I soon reach Four Corners Road.

I pay the recreational fee and park Shadowfax. Soon I'm taking tired steps to the famous Four Corners

Monument in order to stand on the factual quadripoint where four states meet: Arizona, Utah, Colorado, and New Mexico. I reach the massive monument embedded in the ground. No one's around.

Alone.

Tired.

I feel nothing inside.

I check-in on Facebook and post an Instagram photo of myself lying on all four states. I enrich the picture with the "Toaster" filter.

I get back to Shadowfax and make my way into Colorado.

25
Durango

I continue east on US-160.

I pass through Durango, where I stop off at a coffee shop called Durango Coffee—it's on Main Street—such a direct name with questionable charm. I order a warm slice of fresh apple pie à la mode and a mocha to try and dispel the sleepiness I can feel growing within me. I try to get friendly with the locals, the ones who take a table near mine. But no one holds a conversation lasting more than a few sentences. And the locals barely make eye contact with me. It is quite clear that no one wishes to converse. Not the locals. Not the barista. No one. I use the restroom and toss some business cards around the sink. On my way out, I wrap a five dollar bill around ten business cards and toss them into the barista's tip jar.

26
Pike National Forest

On the road.

I hop back into Shadowfax and continue farther northeast on US-160, deeper into Colorado. After a couple of hours of listening to my road music, I click off the stereo when I notice rain abruptly pounding upon Shadowfax. I can hardly see through the windshield. I turn the wipers on full speed and peer through the dense windshield with difficulty. In the distance, I can barely make out the dark gray skies getting thicker, pushing away the sunlight.

This is all happening quite quickly. I turn the windshield defroster on for better clarity. I dutifully peer ahead and I squint behind—very few cars are out on the road. I turn on my headlights and steady my focus.

Rain showers.

Lightning.

Anger.

Aggressive rain and the big bully wind seem to be testing Shadowfax pretty hard. I continue to steady myself, even dropping my speed by ten miles per hour. I go on like this for almost an hour. A few cars pass me. I want to stop off on the side of the road and allow the brute weather to pass—but I choose to press on.

About a half hour later, I'm through it all. The gray skies begin to slowly dissipate. Close to an hour after the harsh rains ended, the sun begins to fully luster as it did before, wiping away the temporary gray sadness of this blue sky. I push Shadowfax faster in order to make up for some lost time.

Hours go by.

It's almost 7:00.

I'm truly feeling lonesome.

I feel like a fool—someone trying to prove something.

I pass on through the expiring daylight, barely making out the true greatness of the Rocky Mountains.

More time passes.

It's now quite dark. I find myself on US-285, passing through the northern part of Pike National Forest, just east of Mount Logan. There's a roadblock ahead. A national forest guard has held up about twenty cars due to the tranquil yet dawdling herd of passing deer. Our engines are off, and we're ordered to remain in our vehicles. I'm held up for about twenty minutes—but I don't mind it at all. There must be well over forty deer passing at their leisure. When the halt is finally lifted, the motorists are allowed to continue east on Highway 285 with a restricted speed limit of five miles an hour. As I slowly pass, I take out my iPhone and record video of some dawdling deer to my left who've already crossed the road but still linger, and then I take some Instagram pictures of this natural moment of awe—using over three different filters. Then, surprisingly, a few more deer appear to my right and seem to want to cross the road. I stop Shadowfax. The last remaining deer pass through slower than the previous lot. I capture an image of a mature stag protecting his fawn as they cross the beat road directly in front of me.

I am so moved.

Once all the deer have passed, I slowly drive on. This image is all I think about for a while as I travel farther along the road. I leave Highway 285 and steer my path northeast on US-85 toward Denver. I shuffle through my music app until I locate the band Tennis, a husband and wife duo from Denver leading the way with their '50s revivalist sound. I play their entire 2011 album titled *Cape Dory*. When I hear the track "Marathon," I really feel good about life—especially when Alaina Moore eloquently belts out the last stanza of the composition—while Patrick Riley masterfully forces his surf guitar to shred chords as Dick Dale does so well—but Riley's chords are truly his own and worthy of study.

I want to write the way this wedded union generates music.

On the outskirts of Denver, I veer off US-85 to get gas and some juice. I check-in on Facebook and post some pictures and a video on my timeline—and it turns out a lot of people immediately "like" both my check-in and my posted images of the mob of deer spotted near the northern section of Pike National Forest.

27
Fort Collins

I climb due north, farther up on US-85, until I merge my way onto Interstate 25 for another long haul. I'm jamming away to the catchy track "South Carolina" by Tennis, this being the second time I've heard this canticle in the past hour. And those lyrics really speak to me, offering me esoteric yet special speculations cf my future. Fort Collins will be coming into range around 10:30 this late night.

I'm so hungry.

I pull into Fort Collins around 10:45, taking exit 269B to

merge on to CO-14 West, also called East Mulberry Street, where I soon stop off at Charco Broiler on Frontage Road South for a real meal worthy of the road. Charco Broiler doesn't close until 11:00 on Fridays and Saturdays, so my timing is magical. The restaurant still has a noticeable number of patrons dining despite this late hour — evidence that this establishment is celebrated and frequented. I feel my late intrusion will not be lamented by the host or the waiter or the cooking staff.

Um.

Umm.

Ummm.

I'm quite ravenous. I order a cherry coke and a savory onion soup with creamy molten cheese for starters. And it all tastes amazing — memorable. For the true meal, I lean toward the Holy Moly Guacamole Burger with spicy guacamole and fiery chilies and rich cheese and onions. Soon the meal is quickly served and quickly devoured. I clean everything off my plate like a good girl. I down the remnants of my cherry coke. I pay the bill and get back into Shadowfax, my pace to the parking lot being noticeably slower now that I'm full.

I pull up to a house just off the corner of West Mulberry Street and Ponderosa Drive at 12:34 precisely. I knock on the front door. Then I ring.

I wait.

I wait.

Wait some more.

What the hell?

I try the door again. Then the bell. Then Maryanne, a

105

co-worker from my journal, opens the front door cautiously in her pajamas, dark red silk. She's dumbfounded as she gapes right at me. This is certainly a cumbersome moment for Maryanne. I may have also awakened her parents.

"Sarah? . . . Sarah, I wasn't expecting you—for another *day* or *two*."

She's still blocking the front door.

"It's Saturday."

"What? No, Sarah—it's actually Sunday. It's 12:30 in the morning. That's 'am'—as in *'ante meridiem'* . . . I thought you were driving through Fort Collins on Monday afternoon. Is that correct?"

"Yes."

Awkward.

Still blocking the front door.

I never called Maryanne to let her know the change of plans.

Shit.

Maryanne fires, "It seems that despite the many ancient luminous star constellations looming over our heads, the lone three stars swirling around Sarah's head appear to fail at connecting with one another."

"That was poetic, Maryanne. You're becoming a literary neophyte."

She laughs. Then I laugh. We hug one another and really mean it.

"I'm sorry, Sarah. Please, come in."

Maryanne finally opens the door.

"One second."

I go back to Shadowfax and gather my duffle bag and

laptop. Maryanne shakes her head and then embraces me in a second heartfelt hug. I need it. I need more. I really do.

She pulls me into the dark living room, twisting on a vintage Victorian lamp that provides our only light. She whispers and points down the hall, motioning that her parents are still asleep. Maryanne then goes on about how excited she is that I'm visiting her at her parents' nest. She explains that she can't wait to introduce me to her friends from high school, especially her on-and-off boyfriend Bradley.

"But all that will happen later, Sarah."

She says I look beat—dragged through a clogged rain gutter of social mayhem. I agree. She leads me into her kitchen and opens the fridge.

"Oh, I just ate over at Charco Broiler."

"I love that place!"

"It's memorable."

"You want some Ben & Jerry's ice cream? It's Brownie Batter."

We gorge on Brownie Batter.

Maryanne begins to gossip about our Superior, teasing the way he conducts himself around everyone as an emotionless bureaucrat who never laughs or never claps his hands or never smiles in earnest. We laugh at his dying fashion of ridiculous plaid tweed blazers.

We chat for a short while longer and finish off the Brownie Batter before Maryanne excuses herself to bed. She brings me a blanket and a pillow—and I lounge myself along the snug couch.

I reach for my laptop just at the base of the couch, and I plug in the battery charger and begin to go a little crazy. I type for a good two hours. It feels great. It's meditative. It's honest. It's pure. True. Wild. My words. Not yours. Lost. Beat. Speculative. Realistic. I recall in grander detail the unwritten events of my excursion in San Diego, through Phoenix, through Flagstaff, the Four Corners, the northern part of Pike National Forest and Denver. Then the Charco Broiler. Then Maryanne.

Clicky.

Clicky.

Clicky.

Then I fall asleep and dream my dreams of yearning.

28

"Good morning, dear."

"Huh?"

It's Maryanne, changed into her day clothes, dolled up and everything. Her folks had left for the day. They set off for lunch and shopping and dinner in the town of Estes Park, just about an hour west and higher up on the great Rocky Mountains. She told me they departed much earlier this morning and wished us both an excellent day.

It's 12:32?

"You really slept in?"

"Yeah."

We both pause in inept silence.

"Are you *still* tired?"

"Yeah."

"Take as much time as you need. Really—take it."

"Yeah," my lips offer in a weary way.

And I close my eyes and soon fall back to rest.

I wake up around 4:40, stretching and yawning and soon standing. I loosely shake my fatigued body, and I roll my neck in a slow circle—cracking sounds are present. Maryanne comes from out of her bedroom, dark red silk pajamas. She must have taken a nap as well. She begins brewing some coffee in the kitchen.

"Want a cup?"

"Please."

Coffee's ready and we sit at the kitchen table and get to chatting.

I tell Maryanne my stories of the road for a good half hour. We laugh and drink our coffee. Though the breakfast hours have long passed, she prepares a once-frozen yet now tasty blueberry waffle. Apologies soon leap from her mouth, because she's meeting Bradley and some old high school friends at 8.00 for a late dinner and drinks afterwards. Maryanne goes on quickly and clarifies that Bradley and everyone wants me to come along. They really want to meet me. Maryanne's told them a lot about me.

"What do you think, Sarah?"

"Yes. *Can't* wait. Can we stay here until then?

"Sure. But I want to get changed and shop for groceries

within the hour. Is that OK?"

"Yeah, I'll just drive around."

"You can stay here."

"No, I'll go."

"OK."

Maryanne comforts me and says I can do whatever I feel like doing. And she means it. We both get changed and prepare to leave. We part ways for a short while, Maryanne handing me a key to her parents' place just in case I get bored and want to come back. She tells me that she feels excited about me meeting Bradley, as well as her old high school friends.

I drive to Rogers Park, not too far down on West Mulberry. I park and stroll off into the center of the sizable green lawn. I plop my body onto its comfort. I love the park's swaying trees. The grass feels nice. I take off my sandals and wiggle my toes into the earth. I open my Facebook account and check-in, soon taking a standard photo of the park to post on my timeline as well. I choose to not read through my innumerable Facebook notifications. I notice, though, that Dragon Boy—the dragon-loving literary celeb—has requested my friendship and has also sent me a private email through Facebook. He includes his cellphone number.

I add him to my list of friends.

The day slowly drags.

Thoughts brew:

Theo Barnes.

Dragon Boy.

McGregor.

Mayumi.

Pearle.

Laney.

Oh!

After an hour or so, I notice the time is now around 6:15. I call Maryanne's cell to let her know that I'm heading back to her parents' house. She says she's just finished dropping off and putting away the groceries, and that she's now off to pick up Bradley. She should be home within ten minutes or so.

We both surprisingly arrive at her parents' place around the same time.

Maryanne immediately introduces me to Bradley with a cheesy yet nervous smile. He's amazingly attractive, and, in a way, he somewhat resembles a well-groomed Chris Hemsworth. He shakes my hand stoically and stares off toward Shadowfax.

"I like your mini-van," he offers. "You're really going cross country by yourself, huh?"

"That's the stated plan."

Bradley pauses.

"Cool."

"Cool."

"Cool," Maryanne offers, as well.

We go inside and exchange a few quick pleasantries. Then Bradley asks of my travels. I give him the five minute version of my road existence, peppering most of my quick narrative with celebratory moments of graciousness toward Mayumi and Laney and Malik from America's Best Inn, and now Maryanne.

"So, you haven't *really* done anything on your trip?"

"I've done a lot."

"Really?" Bradley softly challenges.

"Well, Disneyland is too expensive—and I've been to SeaWorld enough times already."

He smirks.

We then quietly watch television for a while. After about twenty minutes of discomforting silence I ask Maryanne if I may use her parents' washing machine and dryer. She tells me it's fine and that everything I'll need is in the garage just above the washer and dryer. After a short while more, Maryanne suggests we get ready to leave. Bradley says he's been ready. I finish depositing my clothes into the machine and pause in front of Bradley and Maryanne. *I don't want to doll myself up. I'm comfortable with what I'm wearing.* I then walk to the bathroom, quickly wash my hands and face, and brush my teeth—finally entering the living room and professing that I'm now also ready. Maryanne says she'll need a little more time. Thirty minutes later, Maryanne, too, is ready to go. I can see where those thirty minutes went. She's pretty hot when she fixes herself up. Bradley better appreciate her. I put my clothes in the dryer.

And we're off into the night.

Bradley drives us.

I'm hungry.

We arrive at an Italian restaurant called Bisetti's on South College Avenue. The ambiance of the restaurant is amazing. I check-in on Facebook. Maryanne's old high school friends meet us at the entrance of Bisetti's, and we get right into our smiley introductions. I meet Carla and Jana, Maryanne's closest friends for about two decades. Bradley introduces me personally to his high school friend named Garrett—who also is blessed with amazing looks. I'd like to compare him to a famous actor, but his handsome features justly stand on their own. He's refined. He's well-mannered. He's smiling at me. Our reservations were made prior and our table is waiting. We all sit together in high spirits and charm.

We order.

We eat fine food.

We laugh and enjoy the evening.

Everyone drinks a noticeable amount of wine— except me. I sip the same glass of pinot noir throughout dinner. Maryanne whispers in my ear that this is where Bradley took her for their first dinner outing. I smile at her and whisper back that she's lucky to have him. Soon the dinner conversation dries up within us all. We pay our bill and begin gathering ourselves outside of this fine establishment.

"Where to?" Maryanne eagerly questions Bradley, hoping he takes control of tonight's social happenings.

"I want to show Sarah the New Belgium Brewery," informs Bradley.

"I love their beers," I offer back earnestly. Bradley and I begin naming some of our favorites: Fat Tire. Blue Paddle. Sunshine Wheat. Somersault. 1554.

We all get in our cars and caravan just over a mile away. Bradley drives into the front parking lot of the New Belgium Brewery and begins a well-rehearsed sermon on the history of some of their choice brews. He goes on and informs me just how much revenue this brewery generates for the city and so on. I check-in on Facebook and allow him to finish his impressive lecture—he's eloquent—and when he completes his sermon I stare deep into his eyes and smile.

"So, you want to drink tonight?" Bradley probes and stares back at me.

"Bradley!" Maryanne jumps in.

"What, Maryanne? She's barely had anything to drink. People don't come to Fort Collins—a college town, a town that birthed the New Belgium Brewery—and *not* get their drink on."

"Sarah doesn't need to be pressured—"

"It is fine, Maryanne. Let's go to a *sweet* dive, Bradley. You pick a spot."

29

We pull up to a place called Bondi Beach Bar at Old Town Square, a fashionable dive with sympathies toward the Aussie style of leisure. We snag a booth near the bar while Bradley takes control of our libations and orders a round of mixed spirits and a round of shots of house tequila. I sit between Garrett and Carla. We cheers to life and good people. I enter into some fun dialogue about American film with Garrett and Carla, and their taste in the cinematic form of art closely mirrors my own. We're in awe of filmmakers like the Coen Brothers or Wes

Anderson or Noah Baumbach or Terrence Malick or Paul Thomas Anderson or Richard Linklater or Michel Gondry or Christopher Guest or Peter Jackson or the Coppolas (Francis Ford, Roman, and Sofia) or Kubrick or Polanski or Leone or Fincher or old school Scorsese. Jana throws in her perceptive thoughts intermittently. And when Jana chooses to contribute, she does so rather eloquently. We're all having a great time. Garrett takes the reigns and orders another round of drinks and another round of shots, this time Patron tequila. I'm feeling pretty good and at ease. Maryanne pulls me aside and leads me to the restroom. She advises me not to drink if I don't feel like doing so. I give her a hug and tell her I'm fine.

Back at the booth, the mood soon changes when our conversation becomes more absorbing and opens up more deeply to everyone at the table. We chat about the apathy leaking from the many over-privileged kids belonging to this current generation of American youth, the numerous kids with dragging feet now in high schools across the country. They're charlatans. We pinpoint that a lot of this apathy is being instigated by their addiction to technology and their unrestrained use of the internet—the very Wild West of today's time. They're a generation dependent on having things handed to them. They're a generation demanding constant immediate gratification. Bradley begins defending this generation, while Garrett and I lead the discussion by playing Devil's Advocate. We all bicker and laugh and agree and disagree until the conversation becomes controlled by only Bradley and me. He soon facetiously crosses the line and blames my disagreeing ways on my alcohol consumption, specifying that I'm unable to think critically while I'm intoxicated.

"You're drunk, Sarah," he contends.

"Are you challenging me?"

"Yes, I am."

"Well, how about this, *Bradley*? How about you and me *keep* drinking until one of us *throws* in the towel? Then, whoever gives up first will be the one to have to pay the *entire* bill."

The table applauds.

"Sarah," Bradley pauses melodramatically and then continues, "I've already consumed more booze than you. You barely sipped your wine at Bisetti's."

I nod at his statement of fact. Then I reach in front of Maryanne and commandeer her mixed spirit, knocking the rest of the contents down my throat. Then I slam Garrett's drink. Bradley laughs and Garrett applauds, as does Carla and Jana.

"OK, Sarah, OK! We're even."

"So, are you going to drink me under the table, *Bradley*?"

He flags a waitress and orders ten shots of Patron tequila.

One.

The table cheers.

Bradley and I are in sync.

Two.

The table laughs and again applauds.

Bradley and I are in formidable shape and primed for the slaughter.

Three.

For showmanship, Bradley slowly raises his next shot.

To mock him, I mimic his slow raise and bang back mine before he does.

Four.

Maryanne whispers in my ear, "This challenge isn't worthy of your spirit, Sarah."

"Thank you, my *literary neo*phyte," I offer back with draining words.

Five.

"Wow! That's enough, Bradley," Maryanne pleads.

He's buzzing quite hard. I can tell. But so am I. He yawns as he flags down the waitress. Bradley gives me the stink-eye stare when the waitress arrives at our booth. He points his stubborn index finger at my face and bites his lower lip. I point back at him with a beat smile. Then I dramatically allow my index finger to pull back as my thumb extends toward the ceiling. Bradley orders another ten shots.

The table roars.

I feel alive and loved.

Everyone's smiling and living.

Music begins filling the Bondi Beach Bar. Some DJ must have set up shop somewhere. The music selection is preferred, a sort of electronic and indie pop rock mix of various beats tempting listeners to get up and dance.

Six.

Garrett grabs both of my hands and says he's rooting for me. Bradley calls him an asshole. Carla casts her vote for me. So does Maryanne and Jana. Bradley flips us all off with his angered and militant middle finger. I squeeze Garrett's hands and murmur in his left ear that I'm a San Franciscan girl. Garrett hugs me and laughs.

I take the seventh first.

Then Bradley.

"Damn you, woman," Bradley quips. "You *win*, Sarah."

I condemn my eighth shot to the abyss of my belly just to keep my winning official.

Bradley then ushers Maryanne away from her seat, flags down our waitress and closes our tab, soon yanking Maryanne onto the petite dance floor and reservedly spinning her like a dance queen all-star. Maryanne smiles golden and soaks in Bradley's affection for her. Carla and Jana soon join them and immediately find their groove with clever steps that are in tune with the indie rock pop sound. Garrett and I are still seated. He praises my drinking capacities, and then he chooses to punish two of the remaining shots of Patron. I laugh at him. He laughs back and begins shaking his head at me.

"What?" I query.

"Sarah, you're *some*thing else."

"In a *good* way?"

"*Very* good way."

Garrett stops his smiling. He sits upright and confidently takes my right hand and escorts me onto the dance floor. Bradley shouts above the melodic and stimulating music. Bradley again challenges me, saying he wants an official Bondi Beach Bar dance-off. Everyone laughs. Everyone twirls mystically on the dance floor.

We *are* here.

We *are* alive.

And we *are* still young.

I made Bradley pick up the entire bill.

Garrett takes me by the waist, pulls me into his chest, connects his forehead to mine, and commands the lead on the dance floor.

30

"Good morning, dear."

But it's not Maryanne. It's Garrett. He's not clothed. I see his limp circumcised extension. He's well-trimmed. I turn away and stumble out of bed. I don't recognize the bedroom we're in. We must be at his place. I change quickly. He's concerned about my frantic behavior. I instruct him to drive me to Maryanne's. I become more panicky. I have a bit of a hangover. I'm dispelled. I'm peeling on the inside. I'm like David—the male slut who cheated on poor Laney. Garrett tries to calm me. But I shake my head and erratically tell him of Theo. I tell him about my job. Scattered words spring out of my scattered mind. I'm purging everything. Garrett is overwhelmed. He apologizes. I scream that I need to go. He gets dressed in a fury of obedience. He takes me to Maryanne's parents' place. I exit his car. Slam the door. Lean through the lowered passenger-side window. I tell Garrett to leave. He wants to stay. I tell him I'll contact him later. He drives off at the proper speed. I meet Maryanne's parents. They're nice people. They bought me some special jam from Estes Park. I thank them. I pull Maryanne aside and inform her that I want to leave today.

Maryanne launches into one of her metaphysical rants about our purpose in life and the paths we choose to take.

I need to get away. I need to find a place of isolation and contemplation. I can't have anyone around me. I'm feeling a speculative burst of realistic possibilities in life. I *need* to pack up and go. I *need* to get away. I *need* Maryanne to cool it. She does. I ask her to grab my clothes from the dryer. Maryanne says they're already folded. She left a note before we headed out for dinner asking her mother to fold my clothes. I grab my clean laundry. I pack my clothes and hug Maryanne. I then hug her mother and father deeply. I'm now ready. Shadowfax is ready.

And I'm free.

I pull off to the side of the road near the Interstate 25 entrance. I sob in an eristic manner, my tears trickling quickly in visceral anxiety and frustration. *I did this to myself.* I fumble my body to the backseat of Shadowfax and toss and turn and further tear in maddening chaos. I sit up and compose myself and stare off toward the interstate, my mind shifting as I do my utmost to keep more tears at bay. I think of the road I've already traveled and the road yet to come. I think of Theo. I think of Garrett. I think that this road trip has been a total disaster.

I've only covered one-third of the country.

I've only made it across the Continental Divide.

I tinker on my iPhone and stare at a Google Map of America.

I slowly sober my sadness and consider my reality on the road thus far.

All must adapt.

I miss Theo.

I do.

It's here that I decide to do something drastic with my cross country itinerary—but it's quite needed. It is.

I get back behind the wheel and steer Shadowfax onto Interstate 25 north.

My intended and stated route has now altered.

I drive dutifully, making my way toward Wyoming.

I blast the stereo with agreeable tunes streaming from my Pandora app. I let the app play for the duration of this current leg of the road. I take exit 189 and wiggle all over until I make my way onto US-20 West, where I find myself wiggling more. I then take WY-120 for about 80 miles, Pandora rocking sweet melodies all the while. I zigzag and beeline and swirl until I reach US-191. After a time, I find myself deeper northwest and back on US-120, now on through to Cody, WY, where I'll venture toward a destination of popular natural tranquility.

There — I'll *sober* myself.

There — I'll deeply *contemplate*.

There — I'll be *honest* with who I've become.

I ease Shadowfax once I reach downtown Cody.

Then I push Shadowfax down US-20, farther still.

I should reach Yellowstone in just under two hours.

31
Yellowstone National Park
(Personal Business)

I pull into Yellowstone close to 7:30, and I check-in on Facebook and publicly announce that my previous plans to cross the country have now dissipated. I state that I'll soon be returning to the west coast. I don't even bother to read the many notifications or comments published about my past Facebook posts. I disregard all the notifications and fully put Facebook out of mind—for now.

I rent a campsite near the edge of the great Yellowstone

Lake. The site is equipped with a fire pit to grill and openly blaze bonfires whenever desired. The campsite, in addition, comes with a picnic table and a combo water spout and drinking faucet. All this will be home for the next seven days. My fee is smaller than one would expect from a globally-recognized powerhouse of a national park. Yellowstone has the sublime natural splendor one craves. I'll witness its natural beauty more deeply soon enough.

But I will barely speak of any of Yellowstone's natural beauty.

You should visit Yellowstone and see all its true beauty for yourself. The natural images that I will soon absorb are for me to treasure alone. They're to be my jewels from the road — not yours. You claim your own treasure.

But I will tell you of the sobering stars you will see in Yellowstone.

That I'll confess openly.

I can't wait to see the vivid stars sparkle with flamboyant winks later in this crisp evening lush with fresh air. I need to get my act together. To dispel my evasive self-destructive ways. To purge the cyclic bore that has infested my cognitive reality. To be able to stand up straight again. To no longer fling my pearls at the boars created within my own cerebral being.

Here at Yellowstone I'll remain in isolation. I won't speak to anyone or make any eye contact. Nature will conduct my long overdue intervention. Nature will be my sponsor indefinitely. Nature always prevails. And being of nature, I will choose to tell no lies.

I grab my spare blanket and get ready to sleep in

the back of Shadowfax. It was a shit morning back in
Fort Collins. It's been a shit week and six days. I keep the
windows rolled down to allow the crisp night air to sneak
in and scent Shadowfax with a welcoming whitebark
pinecone aroma. It's not too cold at all. It's just right. Above
me the stars gape down and twinkle their marvelous
smiles at all who stare back at them. And I'm one of them
right now.

Ahhh.

I sleep well.

No silly dreams at all.

I awake around 9:00 in the morning and I sit at the
picnic table and face the spacious lake of dark pearly blue.
Then I sit and contemplate my place and purpose in life
for a long while. I think deeply and true. I then go into
Shadowfax and gather the remaining business cards and
flyers advertising my writing. I toss them all into a nearby
receptacle where they belong. I walk back to Shadowfax
and find an unopened water bottle near the back—and
I instantly remember that this was the very water bottle
McGregor pushed into my hands back in San Francisco.
I open this bottle and fully quench my sleepiness, and I
roll a previously undiscovered eye booger into a ball,
flicking it down toward the beautiful earth. I decide to call
McGregor and smooth out any tension. He answers his
cellphone immediately.

McGregor:

He pleads for my forgiveness about

earlier in the week when he kissed me. He tells me of the hypnotic infatuation he has for me, how I've been on his mind for quite some time. I barge into his many soft and flattering words and let him know that true love cannot happen between us. McGregor becomes slowly quiet as his mind fully fathoms my stance. I then forgive him. And I mean it. His mood soon changes into civil banter. I quickly change the subject and inquire about his resignation at the journal. He informs me that our Superior was continuously being a total douche and unfairly criticized him for the last time. He said he's now planning on occupying an open entry-level position as an assistant to a paralegal in his father's firm. I tell him I'll miss him. I promise him I'll keep in touch—and I mean both statements when I say them. We talk and talk. Soon, it feels as if everything is resolved between us. We end our conversation with words of hope and kindness.

I then decide to call Dragon Boy, another person allegedly mystified with me. I can't keep putting him off, regardless of our past situation that could have cost me my job. I need to find out what his agenda may be. I think I know.

Dragon Boy:

> Dragon Boy answers immediately, as well. He's been stalking me on Facebook. He's even read all of my posts since I first joined Facebook back in 2008. He talks of all the intriguing things I've recently posted on Facebook. He then asks why I decided to (1) take on a road trip alone and (2) why I've altered my set plan of crossing the entire country. I dodge both of his interrogations and ask him why he's interested in me. He can't say, meaning either (1) he lacks the skills needed to explain his feelings properly or (2) he's unable to articulate the genesis of his interest in me. Both of my judgments are probably accurate. He returns to his ponderings on my road trip, wondering where the road will take me next. I tell him Seattle, to see my good friend Yasmine. He wants to meet me in Seattle. He asks me a second time, even though I clearly

heard his query when he first asked. He promises me that if we do meet he will not even bring up drinking alcohol. Despite his inappropriate quip, I can't help but slightly giggle. I change the subject and end the conversation in civil obedience.

I need to speak with Theo.

Theo doesn't pick up his cellphone or his house phone. I leave him a similar message on both of his voice messaging systems: I tell him I have a problem with alcohol—a serious problem. I tell him I need help. I repeat it again and again in both messages, my voice cracking into teary melancholy. I tell him I miss him, my words impregnated with a growing sense of truth. I end both voicemails feeling low, like an untrusting whore of a human being—a busted tulip.

I then phone Mayumi and Laney and divulge my full story of the road, the sober truth. They both react with shock and sympathy and promises of contrition, each of them offering support and welcomed words of assurance.

I should call the editor of *Illogical Fallacy*, but I now

feel no desire. If they publish my poem—wonderful. If they pass—then they pass.

It's getting close to the afternoon and my spent body desperately needs nourishment. I drive to a mini-grocery store near the place where I registered for the campsite. I buy a half-loaf of whole-grain bread to go well with the Estes Park jam Maryanne's parents generously gave me, as well as some bottled drinking water and fruits and non-refrigerated meats like smoked sausage and beef jerky, and then a week's worth of pine firewood to burn later during the nights.

I get back to my campsite and delve into the water and fruits. Then I again choose to sit at the picnic table and stare off, again absorbing the lake's stunning luster that I will not describe to you. I soon decide it's time to call every person I am still scheduled to meet later on the road. It's been overdue.

My old co-worker, Barbara, in Oklahoma City calls me harsh names that rhyme with one another before she hangs up on me in savage annoyance—she's always been the brute reactionary; Jenna, my darling and sexy aunt in Houston, reassures me and tells me all will be fine in the end; my friend of a friend Dina in New Orleans laughs and laughs and laughs at me, soon complaining and questioning my choice to only inform her now that I will not be visiting—and she furthers her rant by admitting that she regrets her decision to clean the house and take me out to the cool socialite hangouts in the French Quarter; my old sexy college roomy Erika in West Palm Beach, Florida, says it's fine that my schedule has altered and she wishes me luck; my other roommate from college named Candice, who now lives in New York, has no problem either and wishes me well on my journeys; and so does another college friend who lives in Chicago; and my old boss from a side job I had back in college doesn't mind that I won't be able to crash at her place in Fargo. I'm still planning on stopping off at the scheduled stops on the west coast with friends as previously slated—I'll contact them each soon and inform them of my unforeseen early arrival.

I then dig into some of the smoked sausage and contemplate everything, my mind wandering and focusing and agreeing and disagreeing and screaming and soothing.

I admit to my alcoholism.

I say it over and over.

It's the sober truth.

Will I prevail?

Of course.

32
(Starlight Observations)

I've spent these last few days absorbing Yellowstone with celebration and reflection, all the while taking dozens of Instagram photos and videos: of me hiking the vast trails with eager steps; of me seeing the tranquil trees standing tall like primordial towers; witnessing the festive wildlife popping in and out of sight; of me swimming like a golden fish in the crisp pearly blue; of me posing near the many sapphire blue sulfur hot springs; and of me shouting speculative nothings at Old Faithful as she spits her wrath well into the air.

And on and on.

But it's the stars that center me most.

The Milky Way bursts with transcendent intensity from our distant solar and lunar and planetary friends— for six consecutive nights. It's as if vivacious diamonds filled with sparkly glow were each deliberately cast into the darkness and scattered everywhere to remind the innumerable onlookers below that we are all a part of something profoundly grand. How this expanded existence was first shaped may never be fully fathomed by mankind's collective consciousness. What does matter to us, though, is how we pass through this life before the diamonds stop their sparkly glow and the Milky Way collides with the Andromeda galaxy three billion years from now or if, somehow, life cataclysmically ceases to exist due to apocalyptic events produced by mankind. The deep twinkly nights at Yellowstone refine the spectacular illuminations of the many constellations and faraway moons and remote planets and shooting stars. And I'm right here under them all. I'm here fancying a nobler and more civil world revolving madly under these non-maudlin stars that remind us of our lofty purpose in life.

33
(Literary Business)

I awake early in the frosty morning.

I stay warm by wrapping my blanket around me. I open my laptop, put on some headphones, shuffle some music, and polish everything I had previously written in my road trip memoir, right up to my arrival in Fort Collins. In chapters 1-27, the narrative of my experiences on the road are all now better refined with clarity. I nitpicked here and there, highlighted and dragged, cut, pasted, pressed "save," and so on. I've finally finished my many revisions and necessary edits.

My music shuffle stumbles upon the magnetic and entrancing song "There's a Girl" composed by the Denver, Colorado band Dressy Bessy. I appear to type much faster while I'm absorbing this track, my prose gushing onto the screen in spectacular awe. There's a fantastic rhythm to my typing, as well. The song soon ends, so I play it over and get right back into my rhythmic groove. And it feels amazing. My words tumultuously fire across the screen — like shiny full metal jackets from an AR-15. The track soon ends yet again. To press on, I deliberately loop "There's a Girl," so it continuously repeats over and over and over.

I'm loving this strange and wonderful groove in my typing.

Delightfully, I'm owned by the song's melody.

I dutifully write and finish chapter 28.

Then chapter 29.

Chapter 30.

Then 31.

32.

After a productive, yet duly celebrated, period of work, I turn off "There's a Girl" and remove my headphones. I peruse my fresh words. In these newly composed chapters, I divulged my recent road experiences through Fort Collins — right up to my very existence right here in Yellowstone in this very early morning of crisp chill.

I *chose* to let the narrative spontaneously flow in chapters 28-32.

I now pause.

The screen is blank.

I begin typing out chapter 33.

My mind wanders and wonders.

San Francisco State University.

Oddly, I start reflecting on my college years and my many professors of literature. Then something quite random surfaces in my mind and sticks—it's a peculiar moment from an otherwise unmemorable class. I soon ponder an enthusiastic inkling—a provocative and viable shift in my memoir's narrative.

I somehow call to mind my vague studies of Speculative Realism from my philosophy professor back in my astute years as a literary student at San Francisco State University—back when I was an eager thinker, one hungry to eat whatever literature was expected of me to study. I can't explain the genesis of why I thought of this philosophy course. It's as if a Greek muse whispered sugary sweetness into my ears.

Ah—college!

SFSU provided my once poorly-seeded mind with the needed tools and strategies to yield a publishable crop of worthy produce now being sold in the literary universe— I'm a paid writer—quite underpaid—but still *paid*—barely making enough money to rent an apartment and live a fair quality of life. I live by simple means.

Speculative Realism.

I Google "Speculative Realism" and research its principles. And I strangely begin recalling many tidbits I was once taught on this emerging philosophy some years back in college.

Back at SFSU, my philosophy professor didn't paint

the entire Speculative Realism picture when he lectured about the emerging philosophy movement of speculative realists whose names I had not heard of in any previous literary circles. He only lectured on what may be viewed as the gist of the contemporary philosophy movement. I remember he began explaining that Speculative Realism was officially dubbed its title back in 2007 at Goldsmiths College in the University of London.

Still Googling, and still recalling bits of what I was once taught, I confirm Speculative Realism—with its many variations—supports a belief that metaphysical realism trumps the central theories of post-Kantian philosophy.

After more web searching, I strangely recall moments of my professor passionately reading excerpts from the complex voices of Ray Brassier, Quentin Meillassoux, Graham Harman, and Iain Hamilton Grant. These intellectuals (among others) have seemingly dug a trail through the well snowy-weathered footpath of global philosophical notice, leading toward their inevitable cultural recognition. In the only class my professor lectured on Speculative Realism, I queried whether or not Speculative Realism had a place in American Literature. He laughed and said that perhaps we can all tease and answer my query with two speculative words, "Speculative Fiction." The class laughed and soon came back to quiet order. Then, I very awkwardly laughed aloud and laughed alone. My professor smiled, walked over to me and chuckled and said as he leaned forward to my desk, "Exactly."

I remember he then furthered his playful ways by

later closing his reserved lecture by citing his only source on Speculative Realism to be Wikipedia. The class briefly smiled and quipped in unison.

That was the viable spark.

That very class session was my enthusiastic inkling.

I would much rather speculate than record or annotate.

I then decide to no longer write a memoir about my road travels.

I quickly call to mind the recent edits in my once-memoir book. I acknowledge that everything I composed up to chapter 32 in my narrative was, perhaps, just deafening repetition, given that the style of my writing may not be anything new. But I still preserve everything I recorded. The past is recorded and will remain—but the inspired surge of one's literary future is limitless and pleading to welcome those who fathom the principal understanding in composing philosophical and speculative narratives, or any such task un-attempted by mainstream American writers of literary fiction.

Chapters 1-32 in this very book were of traditional prose.

Chapters 33 and on will be of literary speculation.

I again Google "Speculative Realism" and study.

I dig deeper into its metaphysical ideals.

It's all so dizzying and alive.

Speculative Realism.

I now continue to write by choosing to compose as one who will attempt to and swim in the complex waters of writing Speculative Realism in American Literature.

But I'll only flirt with it—I won't be a champion of the movement. And I'm certain what I will construct will not be of high academic merit—but at least I'll try to write in such a possibly esoteric manner, albeit a decent manner.

And I begin the arduous task immediately.

I write.

I write aggressively.

I even laugh at my silly seriousness while I'm writing.

I speculate the road to come. I fictionalize. I fantasize. I speculate my road experiences yet to come. I dizzy my prose with metaphysics of a possible future perhaps soon to come.

My laptop soon runs low on battery life.

I enter Shadowfax and fire her engine, plugging a 300W car cigarette lighter Power AC 110V Converter Adapter with USB Port into Shadowfax's lower dash. I had stowed this in my duffle bag knowing very well that I might need to rely on car engine power to recharge my iPhone or laptop at some point.

I was correct.

New power's surging within the laptop battery.

I continue to speculate the dialogues and events I may encounter on the road in the very immediate future. I write unceasingly, unless I need to stretch or urinate or nibble on a piece of fruit or beef jerky or bread with jam from Estes Park. I'm wired into this speculative and fictionalized world offering realistic events yet to be experienced.

I finish a dry yet belly-filling chapter in Butte, Montana. I finish a personal and innocently nude chapter in Spokane, Washington. I get free stuff and put my foot down in Seattle. I get pressured in Portland, Oregon, and then later become a silly film critic. Then, for San Francisco and the apocalyptic resolution, I compose a believable hope that Theo takes me back into his arms and runs his fingers through my hair and irons out the metaphysical pains in my perceptive being. I hope that Theo will accept me as I am.

I wrap up my closing chapter—chapter thirty-nine.

I write a poetic piece for my Epilogue, a decent Appendix discussing my review of a popular Ridley Scott sci-fi film, and an honest Acknowledgments section, where I thank those who've made this book possible.

And I'm done!

Over thirty thousand words of story.

The day continues to pass and early evening is upon me. And soon the moon will usher in the thick darkness and the innumerable sparkly glows that will hover above in hypnotic, twinkly awe. My fingers hurt only a bit as they continue to compose words that are true and honest and clean.

Bradley was right—I haven't really done anything on the road. Therefore, as I further toward my writing's end, I revise and edit my newly composed narratives in Butte and Spokane and Seattle and Portland and San Francisco, tightening and cleaning my prose to make them more refined.

I then read for harsh, dutiful hours.

I read the entire manuscript, tightening my prose even more.

It's now deep into a handful of minutes prior to midnight.

No more literary workshop.

I'm done.

Revised.

Edited.

Read.

Finished.

My first book.

My planned child.

Now, I will give it a title.

And I'll call it *Under These Stars*.

I leap out of Shadowfax and reach my well-worked fingers toward the stars that shine down for all in this contemplative world of selective ideals. The stars linger in their lasting dance of dazzling and sparkling existence, their sparkly glow.

I go back into Shadowfax and pick up my phone. I open Facebook with the mind to post this addicting first true literary accomplishment of mine—my *first* book! But then I choose not to post a single thing. I pause and look at the stars. Next, rather, I become inquisitive and catch up on one Facebook post that has seemed to have secured massive traffic.

This is the first time I've checked my Facebook in many sobering days. It seems I have over three hundred notifications. And I come to notice one hundred seventy-three people have "liked" my Facebook check-in at Yellowstone, and many have commented on this very post. I catch up on reading their messages:

Gary Gongwer	Whaaaaaat!? This does not compute. (3 "likes")
Barbara Lee	lol you flake enjoy the rest of you're trip dont get arrested or crash your car
David Yerkes	be sure to write.
Dina Munroe	well said @Barbara
Joseph Rivera	@Barbara ^^^ DISLIKE ^^^ WTF! (2 "likes")
Lucio Vazquez	let the Spirit guide you (3 "likes")
Kathy Kyle	be safe
Peter Peabody	Go cross country! Do it!
Mike Bucci	@Barbara . . . You voodoo smelly pirate wench with holey poopy-stained underwear (13 "likes")
Matt Jennings	Jaaaaaaaam! (3 "likes")
Anna Misra	what . . . keep going!
Karen Sassey	I still owe you a white chocolate mocha. You were always right about the caramel macchiato. I'm sorry. I

am. You're the best!

Courtney Frost There must be a good story.

Candice Napier it's wine o'clock, my dear. be safe.
(3 "likes")

Paul Fraher WUSSY!
(4 "likes")

Andrea Pollera TFS! What's the move now?
(1 "like")

Mayumi Carr Oh, baby! What happened? Call me!
(3 "likes")

Ashley Richards you're living la vida loca. DEUCES!
(2 "likes")

Maryanne Ray Miss you! Miss you! Miss you!

Dave Baptist Yeah, you went to SFSU alright. Gator done!

Diana Rice I'll tell the Bako crowd.

Bev Esposito smh be safe

Angie Herrera You deserve some time by the pool!

David Bible have a brew for me.

Logan Irons Wow. The Dudette Abides.
(3 "likes")

John Petry	You dishonor San Francisco. Keep going!
Natal Moreira	Write a book about it. Have your lead character be a sexy Portuguese woman.
Barb Williams	You'll still love the road.
Maya Misra	Well, that sucks . . . Namaste.
D.Gutierrez	SHIT HAPPENS! (2 "likes")
Jordy Krohn	take lots of pics. live it up girl
Rachel Williams	You better stop by Cody!
Angelo Delfino	Sarah, that girl!
Megan Toby	Take care on the road, Sarah.
Pimp Freud	Stone cold perfect, Sarah Sar. Be safe, homegirl.
Candice Vega	Sucks! Come play me on Word With Friends. @freakyfire (2 "likes")
Ray Succre	u fucker. don't chicken out. (7 "likes")

I notice Dragon Boy has emailed me through Facebook and queried the status on calling Yasmine in Seattle. I realize I never called Yasmine. I call Yasmine's cellphone immediately despite the very late hour and she surprisingly picks up and apologizes—laughter quickly jetting out and interrupting her words which all appear to not possess any fatigue whatsoever. I've partied a few times in Seattle with Yasmine. She knows her city's hotspots. Yasmine then tells me Chicago has been a mad blur. Yasmine has connected with family and friends and has celebrated every night throughout most of the festive town. She then slows her tales of Chicago and mentions that she saw my Facebook post at Yellowstone, on canceling the east coast stretch of my road trip. I ask her if she'll be in Seattle in two night's time. She says no. She says she's flying back the very morning I was previously scheduled to arrive in Seattle, roughly six days from now. Yasmine apologizes and means it. She jokes that she would not have a problem if I broke in to her place and made myself a nest. I commend her jest with superfluous laughter.

34
Butte

I leave Yellowstone the next morning just a little after 10:30. I let the Pandora app control my road music. Once I'm well deep onto US-287 north I stop off at a gas station and fill-up Shadowfax. Before I take to the road again, I purchase some cold juice and phone my friend Erin in Portland. Erin answers her cellphone and states that she's totally fine with the change of schedule, and she wants me to drive safe. I should be arriving in Portland in three nights.

I then call Dragon Boy and tell him I will not be lodging with Yasmine due to her unavailability. I tell Dragon Boy that my expected arrival in Seattle is in two nights. He wants to meet me there. I ask him why. He tells me I'm important to him. I laugh and label him a liar. He says he wants to see my smile again. I call him an asshole. He offers to rent me my very own suite in a respected high-rise downtown hotel. He says flowers will await me in my new room. He says he will not attempt any physical contact or pressure me with any agenda of forming any sort of relationship other than what we currently have now. He says he'll make the reservations immediately after we end the call.

"What will your parents think?"

"I've already received their clearance. I've told them all about you. How special you are. How I've never met anyone as genuinely *universal* as you."

I tell him to book me my own room—no strings attached—and to forward me the hotel registration information within the hour. He does in twenty minutes. He emails me the hotel information. It's all prepared. We'll be staying at the Westin Hotel in downtown Seattle, a well-reviewed hotel of fine culture. I subsequently text him to not try and attempt to communicate with me until we see each other in Seattle—meeting first in the hotel lobby—in just two nights. He promises me he'll listen to my complete story. And he swears he's there for me.

I further myself north and eventually merge onto Interstate 90, soon pulling into Butte just before 2:00 on this clear and commodiously blue sky afternoon. I'm feeling better about myself and my past troubles.

Yellowstone was my special place for deep reflection.

Deep sobriety.

Deep existence.

Deep speculation.

I become hungry and choose to pull off I-90 and scavenge some grub. I find myself driving into the parking lot of a Perkins Restaurant & Bakery on Harrison Avenue. It's a fine establishment, serving mostly classic American dishes unmatchable in price and quality. I order the Triple Decker Club with a chocolate malt and glass of ice water. It was some real good food, *real* American and real tasty.

And I'm back on the road by 3:10, barreling faster now toward Washington State.

35
Spokane

Back in the Pacific Standard Time zone, I arrive in Spokane closer to 8:10 in the evening. It's so cool to coast west along Interstate 90 and see downtown Spokane and all the city lights illuminating the streets. There's an astonishing gleam in that sight. I exit I-90 and wander the city roads, downtown and beyond, eventually stopping off at a random department store to spoil myself and purchase some beauty products to use when I finally bathe.

I cruise the town a bit more, grabbing a quick nibble at

a local hamburger spot on East 3rd Avenue. Directly after my quick and filling meal, I check-in to a newly renovated Days Inn hotel a bit more west on 3rd Avenue. Despite my late arrival, there are some rooms still available. I score a sweet lodging with a queen-sized bed for about sixty-five dollars per night.

I enter the room and toss my duffle bag on the sizable bed, soon closing the blinds and turning on all the lights. I flick the television on for mere background noise.

I bare my entire skin to the empty room and examine my body in the large vertical mirror fixed to the outside of the bathroom door. I deepen my gaze at my nude body just like I did back when I was in fourth grade. I place my right forearm over my chest, concealing my breasts, while my left hand dutifully covers my well-trimmed pubic region. Many people have seen me in the nude. People have said I'm beautiful. People may have gossiped about my features, possibly saying foul things. Garrett has seen me exposed. I wonder if he's thinking of me this very moment.

I do wonder.

I enter the bathroom and turn on the lights. I don't stare at myself in the bathroom mirror as I pass. The floor is quite cold. I bend over and prepare the spacious tub with tolerable heated water. I gather the feminine beauty products I purchased from the department store and pour them into the bath. The hot and gushing bathwater mingles and plays with the oils and the sea salt and the soap crafted by some Parisian beauty product designer I've never heard of before. My spent body has labored and my spirit has endured constant challenge. I bathe meditatively, quietly guiding my mind into a speculative world where fictitious ramblings morph into dialogues and events of realistic wonder.

36
Seattle

I rest well into the gray and sleepy morning. I then awaken and make use of the modest continental breakfast offered in the lobby of the hotel. I make my way back into my room and lounge in the comfy bed—watching cable programming for a couple of hours until moments before my expected checkout at noon. I phone the front desk and query whether or not I may have a late checkout. The front clerk says that he's able to extend my stay until 2:00 the latest. I thank him graciously and soon return to my cable television viewing.

At 2:10, I fill-up Shadowfax and grab a bite for the road at a nearby Subway sandwich shop.

Off to Seattle.

I press west along Interstate 90. About two hours into the drive, I pull off at a rest stop and phone Dragon Boy. I tell him I should be arriving at the Westin Hotel in less than three hours. He tells me he's already here and will eagerly await my arrival.

I pull into Seattle just before 7:00, making my way toward the Westin on 5th Street, right in downtown Seattle. I enter the hotel lobby and dart toward a bathroom where I freshen up and prepare myself.

I'm not eager to see Dragon Boy, but his generosity with my lodging is needed. I don't know anyone in Seattle except for Yasmine. I phone Dragon Boy. He meets me moments later in the hotel lobby—his *parents* right at his side.

He hands me a card to access my own room. His parents immediately introduce themselves and facetiously state that they've heard a lot about me. I don't respond with words or smiles. They then apologize for the events that transpired weeks back with my journal. They ask me to consider what I would have done if I had been in their shoes. I respond by saying that we should all be gracious that pictures of him drinking alcoholic beverages didn't end up on the internet. The father smiles at me and nods. The mother then apologizes if they appeared to be reactionaries and such. I take nothing they say seriously. I only smile my surprised smile at their presence in Seattle.

I immediately decide to unload my belongings from Shadowfax after we have dinner. I don't feel the need to change clothes, so we leave instantly. I demand we take separate cars. We then all make our ways to the Metropolitan Grill in downtown, just at Second Avenue and Marion Street, a sensational steakhouse pushing high quality dishes worthy of every penny. But I order a steak of yellowfin tuna instead. His parents try their best to lighten the atmosphere—and it seems everyone loves me.

Dinner's over.

None of us are tired.

Dragon Boy suggests we go to the top of Space Needle.

It's beautiful. I can see the sparkly stars above us and those gleaming city lights below. Dragon Boy reaches for my hand and tells me he likes me. I let go of his hand and walk away, telling him it can never work out after what his parents had put me through. He tells me they're controllable, and they'll never attack me again.

"You let them call my job and harass me."

"Sorry."

"I'm over it."

We soon leave and Dragon Boy suggests to the group that we all grab a Starbucks coffee and then soak in a late movie before we go back to our separate hotel rooms for the night. We all agree, making our way to a downtown movie theater near one of the many Starbucks locations. After our caffeine fix, we stroll into the Regal Meridian 16 movie theater on 7th Avenue.

But to be honest, my alcoholic instincts now pop

into mind. I want to experience the nightlife popping throughout the hip neighborhoods of Seattle, but I know continuing down that inebriated route will only confuse my goal of full sobriety.

A movie will be fine.

Dragon Boy begs us all to watch *That's My Boy*, the new Adam Sandler comedy. No one disagrees. His parents sit a few rows behind us. The movie begins to project upon the large screen. Dragon Boy is absorbed the entire time, only speaking to me when he offers popcorn. The movie is everything I thought it would be. I tolerate the script's crass, bathroom humor. I become highly offended during the bachelor party scene. But I do find myself giggling intermittently—and sometimes wildly with little control. Vanilla Ice really added to the film.

I soon open Twitter and lazily tweet, "#ThatsMyBoy was mediocre at best. #AdamSandler offered his audiences nothing new, while #VanillaIce stole the show."

After the movie, his mother and father pull me aside while he uses the restroom in the movie theater lobby. They thank me for the amazing interview my journal recently published. They sing my praises and again become apologetic. I make no move for a resolve between us. I merely allow them to speak while I listen.

His mother then expresses the interest her son really has for me. She says that he's even gone as far as fancying the two of us entering into a relationship that will hopefully grow into an important union. She expresses amusement and beams her bright white smile and says that sometimes an awkward situation in a person's life brings about a happy ending.

I pause and stare deeply into her soul—quite stoically, my eyes penetrating her eyes.

"Sorry," I inform her, "but I don't date boys under the age of twenty-one."

His father reservedly chuckles to himself and nods his kudos toward me, "Touché."

"You insolent brat—" his mother cautiously begins to opine with sharp words. "Who do you—my son has been kind to you—and you think—my *goodness*—and my son truly cares for you—why, I don't know—he wants to know you—he wants to care deeply for you—to *provide* for you—"

"No one I barely know will *ever* provide for me."

"He's *provided* a place for you to sleep tonight."

The father calmly pulls his wife a bit to the side, and the two engage in dialogue I can only ascertain is heated.

Dragon Boy—thanks to the high interest of readers in his fantasy world of dragons and goblins and knights and so on—may be a self-made millionaire, a young man of means and security, but there can never be anything between us given our recent history. His mother's claims about his alleged feelings for me are fleeting and juvenile. I can care less if he can buy me a house and "provide" for me.

I walk away from them and head back to Shadowfax. Dragon Boy's mother fires arrows of excitable words at my back as I walk away—her cackling is deafening.

I know this is extremely rude.

I know I should at least say goodbye to Dragon Boy.

I know Dragon Boy paid for my meal, entertainment, and lodging.

But I'm over this situation. His mother is *too* much. I enter Shadowfax and scroll through my music app playlists and soon blast Seapony's catchy track "Go Away." I drive off into the sparkly glow of downtown Seattle.

Dragon Boy begins texting me and calling me.

I don't answer.

I delete each message.

Then I unfriend him on Facebook.

I decide to spend a little bit of time cruising through the cool neighborhoods of Seattle, places like Northgate, Belltown, SODO, Capitol Hill, Pioneer Square, Queen Anne, Ballard, and well beyond. That old habitual and drunken part of me wishes we'd rather have checked out Tini Bigs martini lounge or Bathtub Gin & Co. or the Sitting Room or someplace else where the liquor flows.

Enough, Sarah.

I end my cruise of the hip neighborhoods of Seattle and head for the nearest rest stop on I-5 south, just on the outskirts of Seattle. I park near the bathroom at the rest stop and toss the hotel room card out the window and fall asleep in the back of Shadowfax.

My failed odyssey is expiring.

37
Portland

Erin used to live by me when I once lived in San Francisco's Sunset District. She migrated north after college and hit it big as a contract engineer.

I awake before 10:00 and use the rest stop bathroom before I tumble farther south on Interstate 5. In the bathroom mirror, I can see just how haggard my complexion looks. I don't feel beautiful. I get back on the road and enter Portland just a bit past 1:00. The weather's quite hot and dry, perhaps just creeping into the high eighties. It's nothing like the intense broil of Phoenix weather, though. I stop off at a Burger King and buy a massive burger, fries, and a strawberry shake. I park near the great Willamette River, just at a small park blessed with welcoming green grass.

It's such a hot day!

I grab my blanket and camp near the river as the flowing waters of the Willamette continue their travels beyond. I gorge on my fast food feast as the sun further beats down on me—but it feels amazing. I finish my meal and open my YouTube app for a short spell and zone out on some music videos. I soak in "Quiet Little Voices" by We Were Promised Jetpacks, and I later conclude by watching the video of Tame Impala's song "Solitude is Bliss," quickly empathizing with its visual contents.

The heat is now getting to me.

I'm becoming quite sleepy.

I need more rest.

I dream.

I dream vividly.

Theo's holding my hand.

He smiles and speaks sweet words.

He caresses my cheek and pinches my chin.

He runs his fingers through my hair and rubs my neck.

I wake up and call Theo. He doesn't answer. I leave him a message that I'll be returning home early, perhaps sometime tomorrow afternoon. I tell him I can't wait to see him. He doesn't call back. I then call Erin. She gives me directions to her two-story dwelling up in the Goose

Hollow community of Portland.

Portland is a shiny gem. It's a town swimming in all of its hipster glory and trend-setter ways and true soul existence. I have great respect for the art that booms throughout this city. These people are wonderful creators of literature and music and cuisines and so forth.

I arrive at Erin's place and become flabbergasted by the size of her dwelling. I bring in my laptop and duffle bag. She opens her front door before I even knock. We hug genuinely and get right to catching up. She offers me a bottle of cider ale as we lounge in her spacious living room, but I decline her offer and cite my exhausting travels from Seattle as to why I choose to abstain. *It's only a white lie.* We dawdle around her place and nibble on some finger food snacks. With the television now on, we enter into conversations about pop culture in America—and then into fragments of my road experiences.

It's getting close to dinner time. Erin orders some Chinese food delivery, and it all tastes great. She again offers me another bottle of cider ale—and I again respectfully decline. We finish dinner and both become stir-crazy. Erin wants to make a bar run. Reservedly, I agree after some prolonged pleading by Erin. We get in Shadowfax and drive off toward downtown Portland. Erin wants me to check out the Matador on West Burnside. I tell Erin I'm not drinking. She laughs.

Erin says it feels fairly warm inside Shadowfax. Erin points to the proper button for managing the air conditioning unit on the dash. Then she quickly presses it. The air conditioning button in Shadowfax shows a "shining sun." I was accustomed to starting air conditioning units inside cars by pressing a little button that either displays "AC" or "A/C" or a possible "snowflake."

I still feel dumb for previously not knowing how to manage the air conditioning unit.

A "shining sun" button!

We arrive near the corner of West Burnside Street and Northwest Trinity Place, our bodies now cooler than before. A tough shade of red is witnessed everywhere inside the dive.

Erin orders a Maker's Mark neat and then points to me in query.

I remind her that I will not be consuming any more vile liquids.

Erin laughs and orders me a Coke.

We finally get to talking deeper about my road trip experiences. She soon finishes her drink and gives me a hug. Then Erin comically shakes both of my shoulders. She orders another drink, this one a double, and she again points to me. I don't respond. I turn away.

Quiet minutes go by between us. Then we again open up dialogue. This time we discuss Theo. Erin finishes her drink. Her cognitive mind begins to shift, now seemingly getting fouled with irritation due to my poor choice to change my previously planned road trip itinerary. Erin gets right into judging my unfruitful choices on the road. She really rips into me. She calls me irresponsible and fickle and adolescent towards those who've wanted to open their homes to me. She's only right about half of the things that plop out of her mouth. Maybe sixty percent.

Sixty-five—absolute tops.

I then calmly place my hands on her shoulders without shaking her. In a reserved and dignified manner, I stare deep into Erin's eyes and demand, "Let's just go back to your house so I can fall asleep . . . I'm still detoxing . . . I'm still *hella* trying my best to hold it together . . . You *understand*, right? . . . You see, Erin—I *don't* like who I am right now . . . I'm now combating this alcoholic addiction . . . Have you *ever* been an addict of alcohol, Erin?"

Sharply, Erin responds with terrible and honest laughter, "Yes. I am addicted now. I am. Really, Sarah. *I'm* like you." Bits of uncomfortable laughter blurt quickly out of her shaky lips.

I laugh, too.

Erin laughs more.

We both know of the pain.

"Well, how about a movie, Sarah?"

"Why not?"

We see *Prometheus* in a downtown venue.

After the film we loiter in the parking lot and call Ridley Scott names. Erin calls him an egotistical loon! I refer to Ridley as a pretentious charlatan pushing studio and distributor propaganda. Then we bounce our perceptive thoughts off each other with words that blast out like tiny bullets from a shotgun boom.

Shotgun-style (metaphorically).

Harsh blasts from a shotgun with pump action.

[**EDITOR'S NOTE:** The following section previously written here has been moved to the appendix. If you are interested in learning of Erin's and Sarah's review of the film *Prometheus*, please proceed to the appendix immediately—the language contained in the appendix is somewhat relative to the final chapter of this novel. In the appendix, one is able to speculate freely. But if you don't care, please read on.]

I pull out my smartphone and immediately open Twitter in order to harshly tweet: "Prometheus, more like Shit Sandwich." I included the hashtags #Prometheus and #SpinalTap.

Erin and I both laugh at each other when we finish reviewing *Prometheus.* We enter into Shadowfax and drive off. We honestly don't despise Ridley Scott—we just feel challenged by the way he probes us to think critically. If it will ever exist, I'm betting *Prometheus 2* will be epic.

Oh, Erin!

We're merely two complex souls in existence, Erin and me. I'm one soul trying to dispel my vile addiction to alcohol. Erin is the other soul still choosing to buzz hard whenever the mood sets her right—which may, sadly, be quite often.

We arrive at her two-story nest in the Goose Hollow neighborhood of Portland. We hug one another once we're inside, and we quietly ready ourselves for bed.

As I fall asleep in one of Erin's spare bedrooms, I think of Garrett and begin sobbing quietly in the absorbing darkness, my chin quivering, my mouth cracked open. I use my right forearm to wipe away the honest tears. And I breathe in deeply.

Theo.

38

I quietly say my goodbyes so I can set off early, just before the sunrise morning when above me will soon loom a golden and rosy-finger sky. Erin is barely coherent when I wake her in this early predawn hour, but she does manage to awaken herself more fully in order to hug me and wish me well. Portland is normally twelve hours of drive time to San Francisco, but I can do it in ten and a half hours. I credit this feat of the road by previously learning how to undertake a clever shortcut in California through towns like Arbuckle and Cottonwood and Winters. I can name more slight shortcuts, but I'm too excited to see Theo. I miss him deeply. I drive for hours. Pandora shuffling great tracks all the while. I text Theo while I'm driving. I tell him I should arrive by 3:00. Theo texts back immediately. He tells me to meet him at Pinecrest Diner as soon as I arrive. My heart's beating. I'm smiling like the sun, my cheeks glowing pink. I text him back that I can't wait to see him—my eyes aren't on the road. I shouldn't text and drive. Bad things happen when people text and drive. My eyes are still away from the road. I want to hear a powerful and uplifting song. I shuffle through my music app and select "Careful" by the band Guster. And I'm floating. I'm beaming. I begin singing the song's lyrics with hypnotic glee.

I want to text Theo "I love you."

I really shouldn't be texting and driving.

I send the amorous text and refocus on the road before me.

My air conditioning unit is on, and the LCD screen on the dash reads the inside of Shadowfax to be a cool sixty-five degrees, while outside the temperature for those drivers unprotected by any AC, A/C, snowflake, or illusive "shining sun" button is a ruthless ninety-three degree broil. I'm not broiling. I'm quite cool. Cool and eager. A cool and eager tulip.

Theo!

39
San Francisco

I take Shadowfax back some days earlier than my rental agreement, pulling up to the street curb in front of the rental agency near Union Square in this late afternoon of hopeful romance. I say a heartfelt goodbye to Shadowfax, proudly and affectionately rubbing my right hand over the hood of her dependable engine. Shadowfax served well. And she will be remembered. I ask a passerby to take a picture of me in front of Shadowfax. I set my Instagram to the "Hefe" filter with proper border frame and hand the person my iPhone. The passerby takes the picture. I snag my iPhone back quickly and gape at the image on the screen of my phone—and I'm in love with it. I wish I could buy Shadowfax. I shout a thanks as the passerby walks off into the greater populous of San Franciscans who each zigzag in an endless workaday-playaday life.

The rental car company actually gives me a credit toward a future car rental because of my early return. And I'm grateful for that.

I hastily walk a few blocks to Pinecrest Diner on the corner of Geary and Mason, the very place Theo and I ate breakfast just prior to my American road trip odyssey. From the sidewalk, I look through a window and see Theo is already waiting for me at the same booth we ate at just weeks before. He waves at me. He's gorgeous. I'm telling you—he looks like a young Clooney or a better-tanned Gosling or Law. Such a smile. I enter Pinecrest and beeline toward the one person I can believe in and trust in and build a family with and renew my vows with every decade.

I see that he's already ordered me a much-needed meal of Eggs Benedict and freshly squeezed orange juice. I will soon paint the insides of my mouth with the savory hollandaise sauce, and my tongue will act as the paintbrush. Again. I then notice he doesn't have any food or drink in front of him. He shows me the letter I sent him from Flagstaff, the one written on IHOP parchment. I smile because he kept it. This is really saying something—I think. He kept the letter and brought it to me—that's a good sign. He *showed up* here and he didn't have to—that's the kicker.

Then Theo martyrs words that blast out toward me like tiny bullets from a shotgun boom.

"How much of these words do you mean?" Theo probes as he slowly waves the IHOP letter in front of my expressionless face.

Shotgun-style (metaphorically).

I gaze into the document and recall everything I was feeling at the time of the letter's composure. It all spills quickly back into my mind and my heart.

I take the letter from Theo's stern fingers and point out every line I wrote that was official and true.

Then I pause and do the same for the sentences I wrote that were fictional but emotionally sound. I tell Theo that my heart was in the right place.

Theo, again, shotgun booms: "*Fuck* anyone out there?"

He booms: "Did you *sleep* with anyone?"

Booms: "With *anyone* on the road?"

The check was prepaid.

I'm an expiring tulip.

No petals remain.

"With *any*one?"

"*Anyone?*"

epilogue

(Unedited Last Stanza in Sarah's Submission to
Illogical Fallacy)

and woe to those women unchecked and uncounseled
those reckless abandons who devolve their merits into
perpetuations of self-centered ideals and unproductive
practices that dry the potential of our true purpose
in existence the very reason why we are the ones to
fully produce life and remain the level-headed gender
continuously shaping progressive generations of deep

thinkers and trend-setting   artisans and healthcare magicians and beyond so woe to those beaten down by life's tussles those defeatists who submit freely to apathetic existence and heave away their unwrapped gifts and well-earned abilities woe to you woe to you woe to you who choose to not stand principled because of your disorientation . . . but hail the ones who face their woes those true women of America who persevere through such woes and hail to the manner in which they each strive to fully attain their life's fancy hail to those women who shape a new path for others to follow

appendix

(Sarah and Erin's review, wherein they dispute
Ridley Scott's claim regarding the non-link
between *Prometheus* and the *Alien* saga)

Then we bounce our perceptive thoughts off each other
with words that blast out like tiny bullets from a shotgun
boom.

Shotgun-style (metaphorically).

Harsh blasts from a shotgun with pump action.

Cock. First shot.

Erininformsme, duringanHBOFirstLookpromotional

video, Ridley Scott has stated that *Prometheus* will not be a prequel to his 1979 tour de force, genre-shaping hit *Alien*. It's also been stated elsewhere that Ridley has mentioned that the only connection to his 1979 *Alien* masterpiece is his use of the powerhouse corporation of the future known as the Weyland Corporation, a fictitious corporation loosely referenced throughout the past *Alien* films.

Cock. Second shot.

I then bring up the point that Ridley used a bizarre siren sound-bite in his two-minute-plus 1979 trailer of *Alien*. If one listens closely, one can conceivably hear the same siren sound-bite in many, if not all, of his 2012 *Prometheus* trailers, as well. It's practically the exact same sound-bite. If *Prometheus* isn't directly linked to *Alien*, then why did he allow the use of the same siren sound-bite? Be original, Ridley. Have someone create a new sound-bite for your new and original story, *Prometheus*.

Cock. Third shot.

Then Erin offers that Ridley Scott somehow continues what has been referenced as the Alphabetical Droid Theory (ADT) by naming the android character "David" in *Prometheus*. There's an alphabetical sequence of android names evidenced in the previous *Alien* saga films showcasing an android. Meaning, in the first film, *Alien*, Ridley Scott used an android named Ash (A); later with *Aliens* in 1986 and *Alien 3* in 1992, both the second and third installments to the *Alien* canon introduces audiences to the only android used in these two films, the android Bishop (B); and then in *Alien Resurrection*, the fourth film in 1997, the third android presented to audiences was the robot named Call (C); there are allegedly no droids present in the two *Alien vs. Predator* films; finally, we ask ourselves, in this so-called non-prequel bit called *Prometheus*, was the android given the name David (D) merely out of coincidence?

Erin spoke the drunken truth and I personally believe it was enough to win a future argument on *Prometheus*, point-in-case. But we both continued ripping into Ridley nonetheless.

Cock. Fourth shot.

I get back at challenging Ridley by addressing the bizarre spaceship command center utilized by the character dubbed "Space Jockey" in *Alien* and the gravely similar-looking spaceship command center used by the "Engineers" in *Prometheus*. They're practically the same set—with a few minor changes. Just Google Image "Spacey Jockey" and notice the obvious similarities found in *Alien* and *Prometheus*.

Cock. Fifth shot.

Erin then finishes by reminding audiences that the last few minutes of *Prometheus* was possibly Ridley's explanation of the genesis of the very xenomorph species contained in all the previous *Alien* narratives.

Too many connections, Ridley.

Sixth shot not needed.

Ridley Scott has just been metaphorically shot-gunned down by two *Alien* enthusiasts.

We both could have teased Scott for allowing the *Prometheus* Coors Lite commercials to run on television and online. But we didn't even bring it up. A beer promotion for marketing a film? Really?

I bet when *Prometheus* is released on DVD/Blu-ray that the special features will have even more evidence of the *Alien* connection with *Prometheus*.

acknowledgments

I owe Rebecca Davis, Lynn Aguilar (Heidi Graver), Karen Massey, Julia Guerra, Jill Gileno-Mozley, and Helena Sousa Rodriguez a friendly Big Bear Hug for their sweet pointers and/or helping me shape my once Macho Male prose into the Sexy Lady narrative it is today. Some literary lovin' goes to those supportive souls who've "liked" my little Facebook page dubbed "Heck Yeah He Writes Books." Thanks to Carl Macki for his positive vibes. And thanks to Mark Weiman, a good man, over at Regent Press for being the first to see something in this novel. Thumbs up to Google Maps, for letting me speculate and see the road through their lenses. And I'd like to acknowledge Rachael Manuola and Liz Wright as being two of the top ten ladies to ever take to the American road. I offer a firm handshake to Graham Harman, a gentlemanly scholar and one of the architects of the modern philosophy of Speculative Realism. And I raise a clenched fist high into the air in order to honor the activist, novelist, poet, playwright, and respected friend, Ishmael Reed, for being a writer who wields his pen with conviction and style. A gracious hi-five goes to those generous souls who've endorsed this book with a blurb. And, most importantly, another Big Bear Hug goes to the publisher of this novel, David S. Wills, a talented intellectual who's doing great things for modern BEAT literature. David, you have humbled me—and I'm ineffably grateful for your support.

Under These Stars *is now published?*

This is all happening, right?

Major Tom, is that you?

www.ingramcontent.com/pod-product-compliance
Lightning Source LLC
Chambersburg PA
CBHW060937180626
46817CB00004B/1601